Incendiary Girls

For Rebecca,

Incendiary Girls

With much love, best wishes,
& joy!

~~KODI SCHEER~~

XX

Kodi Sch

(signing #4)

New Harvest · Houghton Mifflin Harcourt

BOSTON   NEW YORK   2014

This edition published by special arrangement with Amazon Publishing

Amazon and the Amazon logo are trademarks
of Amazon.com, Inc., or its affiliates.

For information about permission to reproduce
selections from this book, go to www.apub.com.

www.hmhco.com

Library of Congress Cataloging-in-Publication Data
Scheer, Kodi.
[Short stories. Selections]
Incendiary girls : stories / Kodi Scheer.
pages cm
ISBN 978-0-544-30046-0
I. Title.
PS3619.C344A6 2014
813'.6—dc23   2013041066

Printed in the United States of America
DOC 10 9 8 7 6 5 4 3 2 1

Stories in this collection have appeared in the *Chicago Tribune,*
the *Iowa Review, Michigan Quarterly Review,* and *Quarterly West.*

For Mom, who read to me every day

Contents

Incendiary Girls

Fundamental Laws of Nature

E LLEN IS CONVINCED her daughter's lesson horse is the reincarnation of her mother. The horse's eyes give her away. And her mother always loved anything equine. Fitting that she's now a black Thoroughbred mare.

Ellen watches Abby, her daughter, prepare the horse to be ridden. Abby has already brushed the barn dust from the mare's sleek body, which the mare — her grandmother — seemed to enjoy. Ellen thinks the brushing must feel like a nice massage. The aisle, flanked by stalls, smells of alfalfa hay and manure and oiled leather. A brown tabby weaves between the mare's legs. The horse stomps at the cat, which Ellen takes as further evidence because her mother didn't care for cats.

"Piss," Abby says. "Somebody took my hoof pick."

Ellen has never heard her twelve-year-old daughter swear (is "piss" a curse word?) and resolves to stop swearing herself. When Abby goes to the tack room to retrieve a hoof pick, Ellen pats the horse's soft nose.

"I know who you are," Ellen whispers. "I'm onto you."

The mare blinks.

"Hey," Abby says from across the aisle. "Are you giving her pointers for my lesson?"

"I told her not to be scared of the brick wall," Ellen says, referring to one of the jumps.

"You can tell her all you want, but we'll see if she responds to the stick," Abby says, tucking her crop into her tall riding boot. She runs her hand down the horse's pastern to get the animal to lift her hoof. "Hup."

The hoof remains firmly on the ground. Ellen took lessons as a girl and knows she could twist the chestnut, the small scaly part on the inner side of the horse's leg, to inflict pain. But it seems a cruel gesture toward her own mother. She's not thinking straight these days.

Ellen rode for a couple of years, and her mother was always more enthused than she was. Ellen didn't have the same unconditional love for horses. She had conditions: after her first bad fall, the affair was over. Finito. Done. The horse clearly didn't have the same feelings for her. So why bother?

"Don't be stubborn," Ellen says. She sees a glint of recognition in the horse's dark liquid eye. The mare complies, lifting her hoof so Abby can scrape the debris from the bottom. The silver horseshoe shines in the dim light of the barn. Soon, they're ready for the practice arena.

The March day is sunny but cool, water dripping from icicles along the overhang. Ellen is grateful for the private lesson—no small talk with the other barn moms. The conversation inevitably touches upon occupation, and Ellen is reluctant to tell people she's a gynecologist. Sometimes she just says obstetrician. Everyone likes the baby doctors.

In the arena, Abby and the mare move at a brisk trot. Her trainer, Bridget, stands in the center, barking orders to go over the ground poles.

"Tie up your reins," she says, "arms out, more leg! Keep her straight! Good. Next time, hands behind your back."

Bridget is a small woman with pale green eyes and a feline grace. Once, Ellen caught her smoking by the infirmary stall. Although it wasn't exactly model behavior for her daughter, Ellen was more concerned about the hay catching fire. Bridget threw the cigarette to the ground and snuffed it out with her boot. Then she picked a fleck of tobacco from her tongue. Both women acted as though they hadn't seen the other, because that was easier than confrontation.

Abby obeys the trainer's commands. Although the cavalletti poles are just a few inches high, they're enough to interrupt the horse's normal stride, like a series of tiny jumps that could dislodge a rider. The mare deftly trots over the poles while Abby makes the ride look effortless. Bridget challenges them further by asking Abby to drop her stirrups. Ellen can tell this is more difficult for her daughter because her shoulders hunch forward, but Abby keeps her balance.

"Okay," Bridget says, "this is the last aid I'll take away. Eyes closed."

Ellen holds her breath. Her daughter has to trust this animal, have faith they will keep moving forward. In her head, Ellen says a prayer: please don't hurt my baby. And if you do, I'll cause you bodily harm, and as a doctor, I have an intimate understanding of anatomy.

They make it through the obstacle with ease. Ellen exhales. Abby grins and pats the mare on the neck.

"Easier than you thought, wasn't it?" Bridget says.

"Yeah," Abby admits.

"Your eyes affect the position of your head, which affects your whole balance. When you look down at the poles or the jump, she knows," Bridget says. "So eyes up, always looking ahead."

Next, horse and rider dance figure eights, starting with large, sweeping circles and making each progressively smaller. It's a lovely choreography. Abby holds the mare back with just a snaffle bit, two thin pieces of metal that join in the middle, over the horse's tongue. With the bit and her body weight, Abby has full control over the animal's movements.

While Bridget sets up the jumps, Abby rides along the perimeter at a posting trot. The leather squeaks at rhythmic intervals.

"She's good today, isn't she?" Abby says as they approach Ellen.

"You're right," Ellen says. "She seems more responsive."

In life, Ellen's mother was beautiful and athletic, a synchronized swimmer when she was young. Ellen had seen the black-and-white photos, the girls' heads covered in slick rubber caps, all bobbing in unison. Ellen's mother had always wanted to ride, she said, but her parents considered it too dangerous. So she collected figurines, spotted ceramic ponies and glass carousel horses and pewter mustangs.

Ellen is not a superstitious person, nor is she religious. But as she gets older, she's realizing that science doesn't explain everything. It's unreasonable and illogical to believe her own mother is now a horse. But where did her spirit go? Nothing is ever created or destroyed—it just takes a different form, according to a fundamental law of nature. Ever since Ellen found a mass in her breast, just a few days ago, she doesn't know what to believe.

She doesn't have time for further meditation because Abby is soaring through the air, falling, twisting, bracing, landing on her back in the cold arena dirt.

When they get into the car, Ellen says, "You didn't have to get back on, you know. You might've hurt your spine."

"No," Abby says. "I had to."

"That trainer," Ellen hisses, "does not know everything. I'm paying for her to scream at you. Remember that." Ellen is on the verge of tears. She knows her horse-mother was trying to teach Abby a lesson, but it's not her lesson to teach, that horrible animal. Her mother would say what doesn't kill you makes you stronger. Back in the saddle. Bullshit like that.

"Mom," Abby says, "it's what you do. Everybody gets hurt at some point. Sarah broke her collarbone and finished her lesson. Alexis broke her hip. And Mary broke her tailbone at the last schooling show but got back on and finished the course."

"Is that supposed to make me feel better?"

"I'm just saying, if you're still conscious, you get back on."

"I'm calling Dr. Schwartz," Ellen says. "He'll order X-rays to rule out any fractures and check for soft tissue injury." After her fall, Abby bounced up and jogged to the mare, securing the reins. It's Ellen who needs to see a doctor.

"I'm fine. It's just a bruise," Abby says.

"I'm taking you to a physician."

"Mom, I think it's time for my own horse. I've been riding for two years now and you know I'll stick with it."

"So I get the pleasure of buying an animal that can hurt you? Fantastic."

"I'm aware of the risks," Abby says.

"Look, I'm sorry. Horses are a lot of work. Are you willing to take on that kind of responsibility?" Ellen says, even though it's a reasonable request. Abby always finishes her homework before riding lessons. And she cares for Tinker Bell, the mutt she raised from a flea-infested orphan, now living at her dad's house. Ellen's ex-husband got full custody of the dog but only partial custody of Abby.

"Is it a money thing?" Abby asks.

"No. We'll go get you checked out and I'll think about it, okay?"

"Fine," Abby says. "Think hard." She pulls at the chest strap of her seat belt as if it's suffocating her. Abby has always been a good kid, an easy kid to raise, rarely moody or sullen. Now, Ellen thinks, the girl is just choosing her battles.

Choice: the new rhetoric of breast cancer. Ellen could have surgery, radiation, or chemo. Or all three. Mix 'n' match, a menu of choices. She's not an oncologist, but she's all too familiar with cancers of the female anatomy.

Twenty years ago, her mother didn't have a choice. Scratch that—she did have a choice: die in the hospital or die at home. Ellen's mother chose the inpatient clinical research unit. In the middle of her experimental chemo trial, she coded while Ellen ate stale popcorn in the cafeteria and drew stick people in her organic chem textbook. To this day, Ellen can't stand the smell of popcorn and is convinced she got into med school because studying became her way of grieving. Or avoidance.

Last week, while showering in the staff bathroom, she found the mass. It remains the size and consistency of a dried lima bean. Like any good clinician, she denies that she herself could be ill. Fear, such a primal human emotion, overrides reason. How many times had she seen a patient who'd come to her with breasts like stone and nipples weeping blood? Ellen could do nothing but send the poor woman to an oncologist, though a hospice provider might be more appropriate.

Her lump feels suspicious. Suspicious? As if a tumor has any feelings, she scoffs. She hates the way cancer is personified as evil. The enemy. It's just a bunch of cells that keep reproducing, fucking with abandon. Part of nature, right? Now she pulls her hand from her shirt, startled, when someone knocks on her office door. It's a clinic nurse, saying her first patient is ready. A routine annual exam.

Ellen glances at the chart before entering Exam 2. Jamie Ewing, new patient. A young woman sits on the table in a paper gown, her legs dangling off the edge.

"I like your socks," Ellen says, pointing to the girl's purple argyle knee-highs.

"Thanks. I have a green pair too."

"Any health concerns today?"

The girl shakes her head no and Ellen launches into the physical exam. Thyroid, heart, and lungs, all normal. The girl lies back for the breast palpation.

"How long have you had the implants?" Ellen asks. She doesn't feel any adipose tissue under the saline. She chides herself for not examining the girl's history more carefully.

"Two years. Preventive mastectomy. BRCA genes." The girl refers to the genetic mutations often found in families with a history of the disease.

"BRCA1 or 2?"

Jamie's answer doesn't register—Ellen can't escape this anywhere. What a cruel cosmic joke. Or was it biological destiny? She chooses her words carefully: "That must've been a difficult decision for you."

"Not really. Watch your mom and two aunts die of cancer. I couldn't schedule the surgery fast enough."

Ellen didn't have the test done herself. She'd wanted to breastfeed her child, and by the time Abby was weaned, she'd always been too busy. Plus she never wanted to be a prisoner of her own genetics. Now Ellen feels dizzy, as if someone has flipped open the top of her head and all of her organs are floating out. She knows the words are wrong as they spill from her mouth.

"Well," she says, "you'll definitely have the best tits in the nursing home."

Later that afternoon, Ellen sits at the kitchen table, waiting for her daughter to return from school. She flips through the prescription pad until the edges curl up. She scribbles "dx" for diagnosis: invasive ductal carcinoma. The back door swings open.

"Hey, Mom," Abby says. Her cheeks blush from the cool spring air.

"How was school?" Ellen says, tucking her hair behind her ears to regain a sense of composure. She crumples the prescription note into a ball.

"Fine. Why are you home early?" Abby says, letting her backpack slide to the floor.

"Bad day at the clinic." Ellen stares at Abby's chest. She doesn't even have breasts yet—no need for those cotton bras—but does she have the family curse? No. Ellen will take it all. She'll take Abby's share too. Surgery, chemo, radiation. Even metastasis and hospice, if it comes to that. Everything.

"Can we go to the barn for a practice ride? The schooling show's on Saturday."

"Of course. How soon can you be ready?"

At the barn, Abby tacks up the mare while Ellen sips her coffee under the fluorescent lights. For a few moments, while Abby's getting the saddle, Ellen is alone with the animal.

"You had no right to throw Abby the other day," Ellen says. "You hear me? No right. She could've been hurt."

The mare stomps in disagreement, or maybe impatience.

"It was cruel and unnecessary."

"Giving her a pep talk?" Abby says, hoisting the saddle onto the mare's back. She tries to tighten the girth and the horse nibbles on her hair.

"Knock it off," Ellen says, swatting the mare's nose.

"Can you help?" Abby says. "This is a longer girth and I can't get it tight."

"Sure," Ellen says. She pulls the saddle leathers straight up, advancing the buckle by several holes before letting it settle into place. The mare groans. Ellen takes a certain pleasure in her mother's discomfort.

"How old is she?" Ellen asks.

"I think she's fourteen or fifteen. She had a long show career before she came here," Abby says.

Ellen's mother died sixteen years ago. If she adds a year in the womb, that sounds about right.

"How much would a horse like her cost?" Ellen says.

"I don't know. Bridget owns her."

They walk to the practice arena. While Abby and the horse are warming up, Ellen approaches Bridget. The trainer wears a long flannel shirt and muck boots.

"We may be in the market for a horse," Ellen says. "Do you think Abby's ready?"

"Definitely. She has a natural talent. But more importantly, she's dedicated," Bridget says.

"Can you help us choose a good mount?"

"I'd be happy to. How much are you looking to spend?"

"Around ten thousand," Ellen says. "Do—do you think that's enough?"

"We'll find something good in that range, I'm sure," Bridget says. She shovels manure from the arena into a wheelbarrow. The sweet but putrid smell lingers in the air.

"Have you considered selling this mare?" Ellen asks, gesturing toward Abby and the horse.

"Oh, no, I've had her since she was a filly."

"Abby does well with her."

"She does. But the mare's not for sale."

"Everyone has a price."

"That's true, Dr. McLeod," Bridget says, kicking up dust as she walks to the center of the arena. She tells Abby to do serpentines across the length of the ring, so horse and rider weave back and forth in a snakelike pattern. The mare is attentive and obedient. Ellen must buy this horse.

The following morning, a Friday, Ellen lies in bed with her knees curled to her chest. She doesn't have the energy to move and wills a cup of coffee to appear on her nightstand. The gods of java frown upon her.

"Mom?" Abby says, standing in the doorway, wearing pink-striped pajamas. "Are you sick or something?"

Ellen laughs impulsively at her daughter's perceptiveness. She says, "I'm taking a mental health day."

"Me too."

"Don't you have an algebra test?"

"Maybe," Abby says. "Maybe not."

"The makeup test'll be harder."

"You knew I wouldn't skip."

"Maybe. Maybe not." Ellen smiles. She'll remortgage the house if she has to. Ask her ex-husband to contribute. She will get back on that horse, dammit, and take the reins. Yank them and go the opposite direction.

The schooling show is supposed to be practice for the horses and riders, but most of the girls take it very seriously. Abby wears new breeches, a crisp navy hunt jacket, and a serious expression. She's pulled her hair back into a neat chignon. Ellen is so nervous for her daughter that she herself couldn't eat breakfast. And she's anxious to know if Bridget will accept her offer. Ellen stands at the rail, watching the exhibitors warm up, and waits for instructions. A familiar arm, covered in gray polar fleece, nudges her.

"Jeffrey," she says. "It's not your weekend. Aren't you working?"

"I'm still on call," he says. "Give me some credit. I didn't want to miss this."

"She'll appreciate it."

They'd had a fairly amicable divorce. The strain of Jeffrey's eighty-hour workweeks, his constant absence, made Ellen feel as though she was a single mother. Besides, even when they were together, Ellen knew she wasn't easy to live with. It was for the best.

"God, they all look the same," Jeffrey says, scanning the arena. "Where's Abby?"

"Far corner. On the black mare. Number fifty-one."

"They look great. Not that I know the difference."

"They do," Ellen says. "She's been working very hard. I'm trying to convince Bridget to sell me that mare. But I haven't told Abby yet." Last night they spoke on the phone. Ellen offered twenty-five thousand, well above the mare's market value. Bridget said she'd consider it but wanted to get a foal from her.

"Beautiful horse," Jeffrey says as Abby approaches, leading the mare.

"Dad!" she says. "You made it."

"Of course," he says, unzipping his fleece jacket to reveal the #1 DAD T-shirt Abby gave him years ago.

"I'm going to burn that shirt," Abby says. "It's so ratty."

"Sometimes the truth isn't pretty. And I can say that as the number one dad."

"Mom," Abby says, suddenly serious. "Will you hold her?"

She passes the reins to Ellen and runs down the hillside before Ellen can answer. The horse is magnificent, even standing still. Her coat shimmers blue black in the morning light. Abby has braided her mane and pinned the braids into round beads that line her neck. The girl spared no detail—she plaited the horse's tail neatly at the top. Ellen runs her hand along the mare's back.

"Be good to her," Ellen hisses at the animal.

"She's just like you," Jeffrey says.

"What?" Ellen thinks he's referring to her horse-mother.

"You know Abby's dry heaving right now. In med school you had to run and puke before every test."

"That was just our first year."

"Sure it was."

"She's not like me," Ellen says, "is she?"

"Of course she is. She's more like you than anyone else in the world. She's your daughter."

"Thanks for clearing that up, Doctor."

"My pleasure."

Abby returns, taking the reins from Ellen.

"You okay?" Ellen says.

"Yeah. I'm just going to talk through the course," Abby says, pointing with her crop. "We start with the starburst and log jump on the far side, do a half circle and take the green and the lattice. Another half circle, over the leafy fence and the oxer. Half circle and end on the near side, the blue jump, and last but not least, the brick wall. Outside, inside, inside, outside."

"Break a leg, kid," Jeffrey says.

"Dad," Abby says. "That's only for theater. That could actually happen here. Give me a leg up." He forms a cradle with his hands and guides her foot into the stirrup.

"Anything else?" Ellen says.

"No. I'm ready."

"You'll be fine. You've trained for hours and you both know exactly what you're doing. You could do it without stirrups and your eyes closed, remember?"

"Okay. I want to get up there and go after Jessica and Smokey," Abby says, nodding toward the competitors already on the course.

"Wait. Your boot," Ellen says, and wipes the dust from Abby's boot with the hem of her shirt.

"Good luck," Jeffrey calls as the horse and rider head for the gate. And when they're out of earshot, "It's not about luck, is it?"

"No. It's not."

Abby steers the mare into the ring, erect and confident. They do a small circle at the trot and Abby cues her into a fluid canter. They sail over the jumps, horse and rider acting as one, Abby in perfect position, lifting out of the saddle to give the mare freedom of movement, guiding her over each fence.

It's over much too soon. Even the infamous brick wall proves no obstacle—it's a clean round. Abby pats the mare's neck as they leave the arena. They wait near the other competitors until the winners are announced.

"Did they win?" Jeffrey asks. "That was amazing."

"I hope so," Ellen says, trying to read the judge's mind. She wants this as much as Abby does. "I need a quick favor before Abby comes back, okay? Feel me up."

"Excuse me?"

"Right breast, medial to the nipple. Let's go to the Porta Potty." Ellen leads him inside the blue structure and shoves his hand under her shirt. He fumbles like an adolescent until he feels the tumor. The smell of ammonia radiates from every plastic surface.

"Ellen," Jeffrey says, "you need a second opinion."

"I don't want to be bald and puking all the time. And chemo brain. Abby's never even seen me with the flu."

"You're worried about Abby?"

"Of course I am."

"Then get treatment," he says.

"What do you know? You're just an ER sadist." Ellen leaves him in the Porta Potty. She's not surprised when the announcer calls Abby's number in first place. Horse and rider meet Ellen by the rail, smiling a triumphant grin. Abby pins the blue ribbon to the mare's bridle.

"Not bad, huh?" Abby says.

"Perfect," Ellen says.

"Brava," Jeffrey adds, joining them.

Abby rubs the mare's muzzle. "Pretty good for her last hurrah. I mean, we have several classes to go, but she was great."

"Last hurrah?" Ellen says. She straightens the saddle pad.

"Yeah. She's getting some time off to be a broodmare. Bridget picked out some fancy Dutch warmblood stud."

"An arranged match," Ellen says.

"He's so valuable they sent his sperm on ice and the vet did artificial insemination," Abby says. The mare nibbles the flap of her jacket. "Hey, stop it!"

"So she's already pregnant?" Ellen says. "She's not too old? Why didn't you tell me?"

"The best-laid plans," Jeffrey mumbles.

"I didn't know you'd have such a strong opinion," Abby says.

Ellen's mother, reincarnated as a horse, is now pregnant. Ellen has a lump in her breast that feels malignant. What else could this mean? Biological destiny.

"How long?" Ellen says, trying to breathe normally.

"How long what?" Abby says.

"How long is the horse's gestation?"

"I think it's eleven months, but I'm not sure," Abby says. "I need to go memorize the next course."

Ellen has less than a year before the cells multiply and invade the sacred spaces of her body, a year before she is reborn as a leggy foal. At least she won't be an earthworm. She has done something right, she thinks, and laughs to herself. Then she watches Abby walk to the information board, searching for the course directions.

"No," Ellen says aloud. She refuses to leave her daughter. She has free will, she has medical knowledge, she has access to the best health care. Maybe Ellen will take matters into her own hands and cut out the tumor herself.

After all, she's seen a number of excision biopsies and lumpectomies. The imaging technologies are more fashionable these days, but only to locate the tumor and take the least amount of tissue. Ellen can pinpoint the tumor without even touching it. And she doesn't particularly care what her breasts look like—they'd performed their function of nurturing her daughter. Who better to excise the tumor than herself? She will take control of her own destiny.

On Monday, at her gynecology practice, Ellen has to deliver the news. The pathology report shows malignant cells on Jamie Ewing's cervix. Ellen sits in her ergonomic office chair, presumably looking over her schedule for the next week, but actually procrastinating because she hates this part of the job. And she's distracted, thinking more about the two-inch-long incision she'll make in her own skin, her medical destiny. After calling her receptionist and asking her to clear the schedule for tomorrow, Ellen reminds herself to have a light meal this evening in case the lidocaine makes her nauseated. She'll have to review the literature this evening, practice all the steps in her head, maybe call her surgeon friend Colette for advice on a "patient" with the same tumor.

She reaches for Jamie Ewing's chart. Such a young thing, such an unfortunate diagnosis. Ellen slumps in her chair and bends forward, resting there for a moment. With her breasts pressed against her knees, she feels the tumor simmering inside. But waiting won't help Jamie, nor herself, so Ellen springs out of the chair and takes a deep breath before entering the patient room.

The girl sits on the exam table rather than the chair, fully clothed, twitching her crossed leg.

"I know this can't be good news," she says.

"We need to do a biopsy and collect more cells from your cervix," Ellen says, "because the initial pathology report is positive." Doctor speak: positive isn't a good thing. Positive equals bad.

"Jesus." The girl shifts on the exam table, crunching the white paper beneath her. "I had the option of a hysterectomy because of the ovarian cancer risk. But I thought I wanted to have a baby someday. I wanted that choice, even if I had a daughter who inherits BRCA. By that time, they'll have a cure for her. Right?"

"I hope so" is all Ellen can say.

"Now cervical? That's not even part of the gene. What did I do to deserve this?" Her face blushes red like an infant preparing to cry.

"One cell got the wrong signal and kept reproducing. That's all. It's not punishment for anything. It happens to the best of us," Ellen says, pointing to her breasts for emphasis. "Welcome to the sisterhood. Now, we need to do a biopsy. Then we can talk about treatment options, okay?"

Jamie has lost it, sobbing and rocking back and forth in continuous motion. Ellen wraps her arms around her. The girl's mascara-gray tears stain the shoulder of Ellen's white coat. She desperately wants to tell the girl that everything will be okay, but she can't bring herself to lie.

Later, when she finishes with her last patient for the day, she waits for the rest of the staff to go home. Without people, the clinic resembles a spa waiting room, with warm, neutral tones and subdued wall sconces. Gourmet cooking magazines line the birchwood rack, because Ellen can't stand those women's glossies. She makes a mental note to thank her nurse Heidi for suggesting a redesign. Her patients seem to like the updated look.

Ellen chooses Exam 1 because it has more of the necessary equipment. Generally, this is where she does minor surgical procedures. She gathers a set of sterilized tools — scalpels, forceps, and the like — wrapped in blue surgical drapes and places them on the stainless steel tray. The crisp white paper lining the exam table reminds her of a blank slate. A fresh start. Ellen preps several syringes of lidocaine and makes sure to have plenty of Betadine and clean swabs. All ready for tomorrow morning.

Ellen decides she'll have a party. Yes, a grand party, with Champagne and bonbons that look just like breasts. Milky white chocolate with pink strawberry nipples. Breasts for all! She hopes everyone will get drunk so she can tell cancer jokes. Maybe she'll have a donation going — support my rack. Or, her favorite: Save the boobs, cop a feel.

First, though, she has one more thing to do.

Fortunately, Abby is at her father's for the evening. Ellen drives out to the barn. She finds the mare in her stall for the night and rubs her muzzle.

"Ready for a ride?"

The horse stares at her with those huge eyes. Ellen is so close that she can see the pupil, a black rectangle swimming in the dark orb of the eye. Ellen puts a halter on the mare and leads her to the arena. She flips on the fluorescent lights, which glow softly as they warm up. One of them flickers in an electric convulsion.

Ellen fastens the lead rope like reins and, with the help of the mounting block, jumps on the mare's back. She feels the horse prance beneath her.

"Easy," she says, sitting tall and confident. It's been years since Ellen has ridden a horse but her muscles remember the experience and she relaxes. And she's been watching from the ground and committing everything to memory so she can help during practice and the shows.

She enjoys this feeling of an animal moving beneath her, a being that acts on instinct and learns by repetition. The mare moves forward at a brisk walk, neck arched and tail held high.

Now the absurdity of the situation hits her: she's riding her mother. The laughter rises from her belly into her throat and the sound of her joy echoes in the night.

Transplant

WHEN ANGELA COMES out of the anesthesia, she asks for a dirty martini with an onion instead of an olive. In truth, she just wants to be healthy again. And healthy people drink dirty martinis—no, *sexy* people drink dirty martinis—and sexy people are healthy. She looks down, with dismay, to see that she's still in the frumpy hospital gown.

"Where's my kimono?" Angela asks.

"Angie," Elliot says, squeezing her hand. "How are you feeling, babe?"

She's been in the hospital for eleven weeks waiting for a donor heart. Now, post-surgery, she feels fine. Groggy, but surprisingly well. She peers over the bed railing to make sure her treasured shoes are still there waiting for her: pointed-toe burgundy pumps, in rich embossed leather, with two-and-a-half-inch heels—just high enough to be alluring, but not so tall that they're slutty. Angela plans to wear those shoes home, walking all she wants without losing her breath, thanks to her new heart.

"Can you help me put on my shoes?" she says, motioning to her husband.

Elliot acquiesces, ever the caretaker, uncovering her feet and slipping off the blue hospital socks. As he wiggles the pumps onto her bare feet, Angela is surprised to discover that the shoes feel roomy in the toes. Her feet are not as swollen, because her borrowed heart is circulating all that excess fluid.

Angela also notices that her legs look darker, a nice golden tan. Even the skin on her arms has a deep olive tone. She assumes she's high on the pain meds and can't determine colors all that well. But the horrid hospital gown still appears white with small blue dots, the university logo on the sleeve.

"Is it the morphine, or is my skin actually darker?" Angela asks.

"Yeah," Elliot admits. "I asked one of the doctors and they think it's a side effect from the Toleruxx or the Axcepta. Might be affecting your hair too."

Angela feels for the wisps tucked behind her ears, her normally fine dusty-blond hair. She pulls a lock from the side of her head—it's thick, wavy, and black now. Taking a cocktail of antirejection drugs was a condition of the procedure. Angela had been so desperate to live that she would've agreed to nearly anything.

She's undecided about the hair, but she already loves her tanned skin—usually she burns and picks at the scaly redness. Angela worries more about the scar. She knows that she shouldn't dwell on the superficial, but she's spent so much of her life looking sick and gross that she *does* care. It's her right to be vain now. For the first time in her thirty years, she looks healthy. Who'd fault her for wanting to wear a low-cut shirt without revealing a giant scar?

"I want to see the damage," Angela says.

"I'm not sure we're supposed to mess with the dressing," Elliot says, frowning.

"Whose side are you on?"

Elliot rolls up the hospital johnny and lifts the gauze from her chest. It sticks to her skin, the goo resembling strawberry jelly. Dark stitches zigzag like railroad tracks, not quite straight down her torso. Her olive skin is swollen and puffy.

"It looks like a train went across my body. And a drunk railroad guy laid the tracks," Angela says.

"You know who laid the tracks out West? Not down-and-out prospectors. The Chinese. They imported workers from China," Elliot says. He's a reference librarian and history buff, even at inappropriate times.

Angela already regrets the railroad comment. She doesn't mean to be ungrateful—she should be thanking God. Maybe her new skin tone will help hide the scar. Silver linings, she reminds herself.

A flock of white coats descends upon the room. The head doctor rattles off numbers and cryptic acronyms. All of his disciples take notes.

"And how are we doing?"

Angela realizes that he's talking to her.

"Spectacular," she says, really meaning it, because she doesn't even have an oxygen cannula pushed up her nostrils. She can *breathe*—the new muscle in her chest must be really working. Her bliss becomes tempered by thoughts of the person who died for this to happen. Probably a woman or young man with a smaller heart, a social worker had told her before. Angela knows she's not supposed to ask but does anyway: "What happened to the donor?"

"I can't give you specifics," the doctor replies. "But you're very fortunate to receive a new ticker."

"I'm just happy for a second chance," Angela says. She knows the risks, has heard the whole spiel before: maybe it won't work, rejection is common, blah blah blah. The doctors don't know her secret: she prayed. A lifelong atheist, Angela prayed just before the surgery, making a pact with God that she'd become a believer if He (She?) intervened on Angela's behalf.

Now she whispers a short prayer: *thank you, thank you, thank you.*

The lead doctor, thinking Angela's talking to him, says, "You're very welcome. Part of the job."

Angela wakes, jerking the IV, and remembers her desperate pact with God. She wants to be sure that He keeps His end of the bargain. Angela's alive, obviously, but the deal was to be alive and *well.* The darker skin and hair didn't factor into the equation, but maybe God is trying to tell her something. Angela wonders if she looks more like her donor now.

Elliot interrupts her thoughts: "Do I still have the key to your heart? Should I have a new key made?"

"Of course." Angela smiles. "I'm still the same person. Cross my heart and hope to die." She draws a big X across her chest, which is painful because they've been restricting her pain medication. Fortunately, she can already walk to the nurses' station without help, in her heels, no less. And she gets to wear her indigo silk robe, so she feels somewhat glamorous despite her surroundings.

Angela feels a pang of guilt, like the snap of a rubber band against her wrist. Is she really the same? She has the vital piece of another human being inside her—could Elliot be right? That's ridiculous, she concedes. But Angela promised to be a different person, one who believes in God, with every organ in her healing body, including the fist-sized red muscle inside her chest. She made a pact, after all.

"Don't worry," she says. "I still love you with every beat of my heart, every atrium and ventricle, every systole and diastole."

"I love you so much, Ang."

"Hey, did a chaplain stop by?" She's worried that she slept through her appointment.

"I thought you're a devout atheist."

"I thought you were open-minded," Angela counters. She has to talk to someone about God, and Elliot clearly isn't the person for the job.

"Touché. To answer your question, no. I probably would've noticed a chaplain. Why?"

"I just feel, you know, grateful. For everything."

"The Egyptians believed the heart was the center of consciousness. When they mummified bodies, they put the heart in a special urn," Elliot babbles. "They threw away the brain. Can you believe it?"

Angela pulls the belt of her kimono tighter around her waist. How could this man, who'd do anything for her when she was sick, be so out of touch when she feels healthy?

Angela can't help but scrutinize the chaplain's choice of footwear: Birkenstock sandals with gray socks, which could be forgivable on an aging male hippie, but not on a female one. The chaplain introduces herself simply as Marjorie and asks how she might be of service.

"I'll try not to waste your time," Angela says. "So. How do most people find God? Do they just wake up and know? Does He or She talk to them directly?"

"Well," Marjorie replies, her hand alighting on the gold

frame of her reading glasses, "for people who grow up in a particular religious tradition, that's the lens through which they see the world. Just as day always turns to night, God's always up there, and we're down here."

If only it were that simple, Angela thinks. She wasn't raised with religion and only went to vacation Bible school to spend more time with her friend Jillian. In fact, the tortured corpse of Jesus had scared her. "What about people who make a more conscious decision? Like converts?"

"You're correct that for some people, they hear God's voice."

"Literally or figuratively?" Angela has been all ears, listening in the bathroom, at the nurses' station, even the patient lounge.

"Sometimes in the literal sense," Marjorie says, confirming Angela's fears.

"But that sounds like mental illness," Angela protests. As she leans forward, a strand of unruly hair flops in her eyes. She has to tuck it behind her ear.

"I can give you a variety of answers that've helped others," Marjorie says, hovering over the bed and taking Angela's hands gently, "but belief is something you'll have to come to on your own. Can I tell you a story?"

Angela nods. She welcomes the woman's touch and hopes maybe the spirit of God will transfer via skin, like a contagion. And she truly wants to be infected.

Marjorie begins: "A woman, who'd previously been a nonbeliever, was about to undergo surgery. While under the ether, she had a dream. The woman was lying on the ground in a line of people, like a long railroad track of humanity, and God was a giant foot. The people had to bend or move accordingly, because the foot had an obvious path."

"And then?" Angela starts to think the joke's on her.

"Although painful, but also joyous, she moved for the foot."

"That's it? I just have to have a dream about a foot and that's God?" Angela needs something concrete and meaty to chew on, not wispy puffs of air. She feels nothing but a vague warmth from the chaplain's hands.

"You can't consciously will yourself to believe, Angela," says Marjorie. "Many faiths agree on that point, as does basic psychology. You can only submit, open yourself, be receptive. Welcome the gift."

Submission. Angela has had to submit to disease her entire life.

Marjorie pats Angela's forearm. "Shall I come back tomorrow?"

Angela agrees because it seems like the polite thing to do. Maybe tomorrow would bring them both clarity.

One of the new nurses—Jennifer or Jessica or whoever—tells Angela they're taking a trip to the rooftop deck. Angela prepares herself for her first outing by applying some mascara and lip gloss. The foundation she used before the surgery is far too light for her new skin tone, which annoys her because she wants to hide a blemish on her chin.

After struggling to tame her thick, frizzy hair for nearly fifteen minutes, Angela decides to cover it with her favorite blue scarf, like the old-time movie stars did before riding in convertibles. She tops off the kimono, scarf, and heels with a pair of Jackie O sunglasses.

A young nurse wheels Angela up to the eighth floor. They pass through the atrium lounge and café to the deck. Then the nurse parks Angela in the far right corner, overlooking the medical campus and river, and says she'll be back in ten minutes.

In her periphery, Angela sees a man with a dark beard, wearing a long tunic and an easy smile.

"*As-salamu alaykum,*" he says, greeting her. Clearly he's mistaken Angela for someone else.

"Hello," she says.

He asks a question in what Angela assumes is Arabic. She feels a strange but distinct sense of love emanating from this man.

"I'm sorry," she says. "I don't understand."

"My English is bad," the man says softly. "My brother, my brother is sick."

"I'm sorry to hear that," Angela says. "But he's in good hands here. The doctors are excellent."

"Yes," he says. "This is truth, *Insha'Allah.*"

Angela wonders if he's trying to tell her something. Maybe he wasn't mistaken and he can see into her heart. Maybe he recognizes that she has a Muslim soul. Maybe God is trying to tell Angela something—He's made her appear Muslim, so she should follow Islam. Angela feels a wave of relief wash over her.

She cancels the chaplain's second visit and asks for someone Muslim instead. On the phone, a woman from Spiritual Services apologizes profusely but says they don't have an imam on staff. It's a large university hospital in a liberal college town—still, it's the Midwest, Angela reasons, not exactly known for its religious diversity.

They send her several books from the patient library, including an English translation of the Qur'an. Angela can't find anything about conversion. Is it really conversion if she was never anything to begin with? Angela studies the pillars of Islam, which include prayer at regular intervals—she vows to perform whatever rituals necessary.

Angela does find it difficult to pray five times a day without privacy from the staff and only a clean sheet as a prayer rug. She's been eating solid food for more than a week (no ham or bacon, obviously), but they want to keep her for further observation, to ensure she doesn't have any more side effects. She can't wait to have a real bath, to immerse herself in water and cleanse the hospital odor from her body.

The gift shop sells an impressive array of scarves, for the cancer ladies, Angela assumes. Since she only has the blue scarf to cover her hair, she wants another option, choosing a raw silk one in shades of purple, cobalt, and deep green, with delicate metallic threads woven throughout. The hospital even has an in-house stylist who comes and helps with her makeup, selecting the right shade of foundation and showing Angela how to apply smoky kohl eyeliner. Being Muslim doesn't mean Angela can't be sexy—quite the opposite, in fact. It's all about the accessories: scarves, makeup, jewelry, shoes. Any harlot could put her cleavage on display. She likes the idea of saving her breasts for Elliot's eyes only.

Besides, after having her sick body on display for years, she welcomes the chance to outfit it in interesting textiles and flowing fabrics. Plus, her beloved shoes are well within the boundaries, as far as she can tell from her readings and perusals of the Internet.

Elliot seems less impressed. He strolls into her room with two cups of coffee.

"Still wearing the scarf, I see," Elliot says, handing her a steaming cup.

"It's called a hijab." Angela smoothes the fabric. She chooses to wear the covering in public, as an act of modesty, but also to identify herself as part of the *ummah*.

"Come on. You're actually religious now? Why not Buddhism? At least that religion makes some sense to me, kindness and love and all that."

"Buddhists don't have to prove their faith in the same way. They don't *do* anything. Was there tea?" Angela says, raising her cup. She's lost her taste for bland American coffee.

"You hate tea. I believe you once compared the taste to warm dishwater," Elliot says, "after the soap's been used up."

"What, I can't change my mind?" she asks. Her husband could be so frustrating. It's as if he has to create a new conflict, now that her health isn't an issue.

"I'm going to talk to your doctors about the medications." Elliot has the same determined look he gets when he thinks he's right, poised to consult some obscure database.

"Why are you so concerned? I feel healthy," she says. She's annoyed that he has to question everything, as if he's suspicious of her good health. Angela can handle any side effects so long as she feels this vibrant and alive.

Finally, after four weeks of recovery, they give Angela her discharge papers. A volunteer wheels her out to the car, even though Angela has been roaming the hospital corridors for days, her heels clicking on the vinyl floors. When she fastens her seat belt, the chest strap doesn't even hurt. The scars are brownish pink now.

"Can I drive?" she asks.

"Let's start slow," Elliot replies. "Tomorrow?"

Angela flips the sun visor down and adjusts her hijab. She hasn't quite gotten the placement of the bobby pins right.

"Maybe you have the heart of a Muslim," he says. "Her DNA is sabotaging yours."

"Elliot," she says.

"Fine. I'm sorry. But you have to admit it's creepy."

"Can we talk about something else?" Angela doesn't want to fight. She just wants to be home, to take a nice bath, and to enjoy being able to walk without getting out of breath.

"Sure, let's change the subject," Elliot says. "Are you going to use a sword to make me convert?"

"That's a gross misconception. Islam is a very peaceful—"

"I know. It was a joke. Not funny, I guess," says Elliot. "Look, I'm not trying to be a prick. It's just that you seem completely different. And you don't need me anymore. You have Allah or whatever."

"He's not your replacement." Angela laughs.

They pull into the driveway. Angela's never been happier to see their bungalow on Summit Street. When she enters the living room, she makes a mental note to take down the photos and replace them with the beautiful calligraphy and abstract designs in her books. And she's no longer fond of the pale blue and yellow cottage-style decor. She wants more jewel tones, maybe a rich burgundy Persian rug.

"No, wait!" Elliot says. "I was going to carry you." He pulls her back outside, scoops her up, and carries her across the threshold. Her foot smacks the doorjamb and she laughs because the pain means nothing. She's home, at last, with the man who loves her.

"Shit," Elliot says. "Maybe next time I'll get this right."

Angela can't stop giggling because there won't be a next time. This is it, she thinks.

"Let's dance," she says. Finally, she's allowed to dance—her new heart can take it.

"Is that allowed in your new religion?" he asks.

"Of course. Just be easy on me."

He takes her hand. Angela's feet fit nicely on top of his, and he leads them in a silent waltz, twirling around the room until she feels dizzy.

When Angela wakes the next morning, Elliot's already off to work, because she insisted that he return to his job at the library — she feels better than she ever has in her entire life. No need for a babysitter. Angela wraps the hijab around her head and does her prayers, fully prostrate. Since she wants to go outside, she's careful to wear unstructured clothing. A loose, long-sleeved tee and black palazzo pants do just fine.

Angela explores the backyard, grass sparkling with dew. In the lilac bush, a cardinal chirps. She stomps around like a child, swinging her arms and startling the bird, which disappears in a red flash. She jogs around the house to the front yard. Her borrowed heart beats quickly, her lungs suck in oxygen, and Angela's body feels just right. In fact, she can't recall another time she felt so happy.

Angela nearly crashes into her friend Tess, who comes bringing two casseroles, a plate of cookies, and a bucket of cleaning supplies. Tess drops the plate on the lawn.

"Do you put chemicals on your grass?" Tess says as she picks up the cookies.

"No."

"Then they're fine. How *are* you?"

"I'm good. Really good," Angela says. She wants to shout from the rooftops how well she feels. If this is how healthy people feel all the time, why isn't the world a happier place?

"What's with the burka?" Tess asks.

"It's a hijab," Angela replies, angling her head so the scarf catches the light. "Can you believe it? I found religion."

"Is it a good opiate, like heroin?"

Angela remains silent. How is she supposed to respond to such criticism, even in jest?

"I'm sorry. Couldn't resist that one. You made fun of me for going to Mass with my ex, remember?" Tess says. "But you look great. Your skin's—um, it's like, glowing."

The sun peeks through the clouds. All is forgiven for Angela's former coworker and dear friend. "Well, come in," Angela says.

"Sure. I came to help out with cleaning and laundry. Wasn't sure how you and Elliot were doing with all of that," Tess says.

To be honest, Elliot has taken care of everything for the past year, but now, Angela can take over the household duties. "That's so sweet. Actually, I feel great. Lemonade?"

"Sure."

They carry glasses to the breakfast nook. Angela sees no need for the headscarf in her own home, in the company of a female friend, so she takes it off.

"Damn!" Tess says. "Do the antirejection drugs affect your hair? They must be really nasty."

"I kind of like it. It's a lot thicker now," Angela says, running her fingers through her curls. Why can't the people closest to her understand? She's happy. She's healthy. Why can't that be enough?

When Elliot goes to work the next day, Angela insists on driving. He's quiet and doesn't even put up a fight about her request. Just like riding a bike, she tells him. And it is—she feels comfortable, even powerful. She can walk anywhere, drive anywhere, take off if she wanted. But she has a specific place in mind.

Back at home, Angela looks up the nearest mosque online. There's only one valid hit, which makes the decision simple. After choosing her best scarf, putting on makeup, and slipping into a pair of black kitten heels—she wants to look elegant and feminine—Angela drives to the mosque.

She ends up circling the block four times, debating whether to go in. The building looks like a repurposed old bank, or maybe a Carnegie library, complete with two stone pillars. She's not sure what she expected—maybe a minaret—but this certainly doesn't fit her mental picture.

When she enters, she's overwhelmed by the smell of wood polish, a fake lemon scent. A mosaic fountain gurgles in the lobby. She follows the signs to the imam's study and knocks forcefully, as if this will overcome her sudden lack of confidence. Angela greets the imam, an older man wearing a long white robe. His graying beard almost reaches his collarbone.

"*As-salamu alaykum,*" she says, hoping she's pronounced it correctly.

"*Wa 'alaykum al-salam,*" he returns. He motions for her to sit. She introduces herself, and he repeats her name slowly, enunciating each syllable.

"I think I'm Muslim," she blurts out.

"Then you have come to the right place," he says, with kindness rather than condescension.

"How do I convert?"

"You recite the sacred *shahadah*: There is no god but Allah and Muhammad is His prophet."

Angela carefully repeats his exact words. She'd seen the oath in her book *Islam for Beginners.*

"Welcome, my sister," says the imam.

"That's it? I'm Muslim?" Angela asks. The process seems too simple.

"Yes, as long as you believe in no other god. What questions do you have of the holy Qu'ran?"

"Um, I'm still reading." Angela has been so focused on following the rules that she hasn't formulated any meaningful questions. She can confidently say that she believes in no other god—Allah seems reasonable. The problem is if she can believe in *any* god. She'll keep doing the rituals, and at some point, she assumes, true belief will follow.

"In the meantime," the imam says, "we can choose a new religious name to welcome a beautiful young woman to the *ummah*."

Warmth rises in her cheeks. She's never been called beautiful by anyone other than Elliot. Oh, she thinks, a new name would be perfect.

"My name is, or was, Angela."

"What do you think of Aisha?" he asks. "She was a beloved wife of the Prophet. Perhaps Abidah or Aliyah?"

The last suggestion might be a good name, since it has three syllables and ends in the same sound as her birth name. "Aliyah. I like Aliyah."

"Excellent. The holy month of Ramadan approaches," the imam says. "You will be fasting, yes?"

"Yes," the newly christened Aliyah says, angry with herself for not knowing the calendar. How had she overlooked this? There was so much to learn.

"Come to our Friday prayers. I will introduce you to Sister Zayneb and Sister Fatema. They can guide you."

Aliyah thanks him, and although she wants to wrap her arms around him, she's not sure if that would be appropriate. Instead, she floats to the car, her whole body feeling buoyant and light.

By the time Elliot arrives home, she's halfway through *Islam and the Modern Woman*. He settles on the sofa next to her, curious to know what she's reading.

Aliyah is too excited to keep the holy month a secret. "Ramadan starts soon."

"That's where they fast all day, right?" Elliot says.

"Not they. *We*. It's one of the five pillars. So I can prove my faith." She'll have to wake early, before sunrise, to pray and eat. Then, throughout the day, she'll abstain from any food, even water, to show her devotion to Allah. At sunset, she'll pray before breaking her fast with fresh dates.

"I don't think fasting's a good idea," Elliot says, "with your health and all. Honestly, I think you should see someone."

"I spoke with the imam today. He was a lovely person," Aliyah tells her husband.

"I was thinking more along the lines of a psychiatrist, Ang. I mean, this is a lot to take on."

"I'd like to be called Aliyah now."

"Seriously?"

"Yes," she snaps.

"Tell me, Aliyah," Elliot says quietly. "You really do believe in God? In Allah?"

"Of course." By this point, Aliyah is both frustrated and annoyed. Why must he constantly undermine her? "You're just envious."

"You're right," Elliot says. "I want that comfort. I want to know there's something greater than me. But I just can't make that leap. And I'm genuinely curious about what swayed you. So can we talk about it?"

"I'm reading," says Aliyah. In truth, she hasn't been able to make the leap either. She's still standing on the edge, waiting for proof that something will break her fall.

Elliot retreats to his study. Aliyah follows him and stands in the doorway, but he remains glued to the computer screen. Literature searches: organ transplant side effects, antirejection drugs, sudden religiosity, personality changes. Nothing explains Aliyah's condition.

Aliyah, née Angela, is somewhat confused about the last pillar of Islam. Should she give money to charitable causes even though they're still waiting for the final hospital bill? Still, they're more fortunate than most of the world, and she must have something to contribute. Aliyah combs through her closet, finding all of her tight or revealing clothing for donation. Then she tackles Elliot's closet, making a rule to give away anything he hasn't worn in the past year. She also sorts through the pantry and produces two grocery bags full of canned goods for the food bank.

Later that day, Tess calls and asks if Aliyah would like to go out for a drink. Of course she wants to see her friend, but booze is definitely *haram*: forbidden. And she's not sure she wants to be around that kind of temptation.

Aliyah wonders how much abstaining from her favorite martini really proves. Or any of this, really. She's been performing all these rituals, doing everything the religion asks of her, but none of these performances has brought her any closer to actual belief. God hasn't spoken to her, she's had no visions of Him—in the form of a foot or otherwise—and to make things worse, she's alienated her husband and best friend in the process. What if Elliot's right, and like him, she's just incapable of belief?

The next morning, when Aliyah puts on her hijab for prayers, she notices that her hair is a limp, pale brown color. Her skin, still dark, now has more red undertones than olive. Did she forget to do all five prayers yesterday? Maybe she ate something with pork in it. Aliyah decides to redouble her efforts by praying at least ten times that day. Perhaps today He'll make Himself known to her and she can truly believe.

Aliyah tries to distract herself by cooking. She wants to have plenty of food ready for next week, when the fasting starts each day at dawn and ends at dusk. The refrigerator is crammed with hummus, baba ghanoush, spinach pie, stuffed grape leaves, falafel, and pita. She's been reading about rituals too, so she doesn't make a fool of herself when she goes to the masjid.

With all of her energy exhausted, she curls up on the sofa to watch a travel video from the library. She chooses one about the Arabian Peninsula. The tour guide starts by pointing out the sights of Old Jerusalem. Next he takes her past the Dome of the Rock and then through the arches to see the beautiful script. She's excited because she's never been out of the country, except for Canada, which doesn't really count. Inside, she imagines it's cool and tranquil. A sanctuary. She finally submits to deep slumber.

When Aliyah wakes after twelve hours of sleep, she still feels tired. Nudging her toes into slippers, she walks to the bathroom. The effort makes her pant.

"Oh my God," she says, seeing her reflection. Her skin is pale. Her hair, dirty blond. She leans into the mirror, seeing Angela the sick woman.

After slipping off her nightshirt, she steps into the shower. Even though the water is lukewarm, she rolls a bar of soap over her body and scrubs with her fingernails. She presses so hard that blood trickles down her legs, but she can't erase the pale skin. There is no darker skin underneath as she had hoped.

Exhausted and out of breath, she sits on the tile floor of the shower. She has to muster the energy for a pilgrimage to Mecca. And what if she hasn't contributed enough to charity, another pillar of Islam? Donating some food and a few clothes obviously wasn't enough.

After she finishes her prayer, she'll go about researching nonprofit organizations that promote organ donation and research. They still have to pay the hospital expenses not covered by insurance, but they'll make it work, especially given the alternative. They also have a rainy day fund, so she'll clear out their savings and give it all to the Donate Life campaign. Then she'll call Visa and MasterCard and ask them to increase their credit limit so she can make more donations. She must prove to God how serious she is. And then she'll call the doctor.

In the specialist's office—she had requested a woman, for modesty's sake—she's surprised to find pink roses in the exam room. They float, decapitated, in a shallow vase of water and she imagines the doctor bent over a rosebush.

As she struggles for breath, they draw her blood and run a battery of tests—the whole exhaustive list. An EKG and then an echocardiogram of her heart. Finally, the doctor sits on her little stool and makes eye contact.

"Angela," she says. "I have some bad news."

"I know." Angela pulls a strand of her hair from under the hijab. It's still blond. She's been praying almost nonstop since she cleared out the bank account and maxed the credit cards, giving all the money to charity. What has she done to deserve this? She betrayed God by failing to believe, and now He's betraying her.

"Your test results show your body is rejecting the heart."

"Maybe it's rejecting me." Maybe, she thinks, she didn't deserve a new heart in the first place.

"This was a known risk," the doctor says.

"What do we do now?"

"We'll adjust your medications and put you on the transplant list again, but I can't make any guarantees." The doctor only has a tan line from her watch—doesn't she wear gloves when tending the roses? Angela checks for dirt under her fingernails. Immaculate. Her pager beeps, insisting on her attention.

"I'll be back in a minute. We can talk more then," she says, gliding out of the room.

Angela throws off the exam gown and pulls on her clothes. Then she falls to the floor to pray, out of breath, in tears, because she doesn't know which way is east.

She's resting on the sofa when Elliot gets home. Her heart feels sluggish. Before Angela can hide in the bathroom or feign sleep to avoid admitting he was right, Elliot walks into the living room. She picks up the glossy travel guide on Saudi Arabia, which she'll need for the pilgrimage to Mecca.

"Hey, babe," he says, leaning forward to hug her. "You look pale."

"I don't feel good." Out of habit, she feels for her curls, but her hair is straight. Disappointed, she smoothes it anyway. Peering at the photos in the travel guide, she tries to read the Arabic characters on a vendor's stand. They're just squiggly lines. The vendor, an old man, stares back at her with a mocking grin.

"Just tired or should we go to the ER?" Elliot asks.

"It's not worth a hospital trip," Angela replies. "You can say it. Rub it in, say I told you so."

Elliot cradles her face in his hands and presses his forehead to hers. "I'm sorry, Ang. I should've been more supportive. I don't *want* to be right, because that means—"

"I know," she interrupts, unable to hear the rest. Her eyelashes almost touch his.

"So," Elliot says, choking on the word, eyes wet. "What're you reading?"

Angela has never seen her husband cry. At that moment,

she doesn't feel God, but she certainly feels love and the person in front of her has plenty to give. She believes in the love that her donor had, the generosity to give someone another chance at life, even if it won't last. She may even believe in the love that people have for God, although Angela herself can't make the leap.

Not only does she believe in Elliot's love, but she will submit to it. She falls into his arms and imagines the lands they'll visit. The mountains of Asir, the sands of Rub' al Khali, and the waves of the Red Sea. She's flying now, looking out the icy plane window, amazed just how far she is from Earth.

Miss Universe

Two hours before the competition, we find a pink shoe box of scorched hair in the hotel lobby. That cunt Miss Venezuela stole somebody's blond extensions—real human hair—and lit them on fire. The hair smells like skin after you twist a cigarette in it. We check our rooms to see if anything's missing. This year, the competition is particularly fierce.

My hair! Miss USA shrieks. Miss USA and her coaches do not have enough time to get new extensions that match. Her roommate, Miss Germany, offers to cut her own locks. She's such a martyr, even though she's the perfect Aryan specimen, with a golden lion's mane and sleeping pill–blue eyes. Maybe she feels guilty.

Miss Israel reminds Miss USA that it's not the end of the world.

How would you know? asks Miss Palestine, who can't officially compete but hopes to tap dance in the opening number.

Really, is not so bad, says Miss Afghanistan. *Is only little hair.*

We stare at Miss Afghanistan. She's the odds-on favorite, only because she survived some crazy bombing. A long wormy scar the color of strawberry jam snakes down her leg. Normally, she'd have to cover it up with heavy makeup, the special kind that doesn't rub off on your clothes, but the judges claim it shows character. The scar is its own antiviolence charity. She doesn't have to say much in the interviews.

It's not real, says her roommate, Miss Zimbabwe, *the scar isn't real.*

What? That's impossible. We rub our fingers across the scar and get bright pink goo stuck in our nails.

Fake! we all scream. *Miss Afghan Blanket is a stupid liar fake! What else on you is fake, princess?*

No-nothing, Miss Afghanistan stammers in her practiced little accent. She backs away from us. We make a circle around her.

As we hold her down, we take off her robe. The swimsuit peels away like wrapping paper. What's inside? Her breasts aren't real either, hard and lumpy. They hardly move. Miss Afghanistan is struggling so we pin her down with our knees.

She needs to learn her fakeness is not acceptable. We'll teach her a lesson. We examine the toes on her right foot, one-two-three-four-five little piggies. Miss Japan has a sharp nail file that saws right through the skin of the big toe and we keep hacking until the toe comes off. Miss Afghanistan howls. Now she has a real disability — she won't be able to balance as she walks down the runway. We picture her tottering like an infant and falling on her made-up face. Nobody likes a gimp beauty queen, especially the judges.

The blood seeping from the big toe matches Miss Afghanistan's pedicure polish. Real blood isn't that bright red. It's fake too. We pick the bone out of the toe and test it, knocking it against the wall. Hard as a rock from Tiffany's. Real bone isn't that durable. Her whole body is fake, one big artificial lump molded into breasts and hips and cheekbones.

We peel back the skin on her foot. Too soft and stretchy to be real. And her skin is orangey bronze. It comes off easily, too easily, and reveals her blood and tendons and bone. When we get to her hips and torso, we find little pockets of yellow fat. There's lots of it around her liver, all of her organs. We've seen liposuction done on TV. The fat wasn't so yellow.

The skin on the rest of her body, including her face, comes away in our fingernails. We put it in a pile next to her so the maid can clean it up. Her scalp is more difficult. The glossy black hair sticks to it. We forgot all about her body hair and we search the pile of skin for her eyelashes and eyebrows. Everything else was shaved or waxed clean. We pluck out the eyelashes. Too dark and curly.

What's left is muscle and bone and internal organs. Her muscle looks like raw beef. It's red and sinewy. Such an elaborate fake. The bone is too hard. Her organs, squishy and warm, melt in our hands. To think we might've lost to this poser. We have to draw the line somewhere.

It's an hour before the competition. We toss her insides on the floor so we can wash our hands clean. Miss Afghanistan has made a mess. Housekeeping, please.

The blood comes out of our manicures with a little scrubbing. We hum the opening number as we scrub and tap our feet to the rhythm. Before we know it, it's showtime.

Gross Anatomy

GABE FOLLOWS ME around the house. He's the cadaver we're dissecting in Gross Anatomy. The first time I see him, he's looking through the kitchen cabinets. His back is to me, exposing the muscles we teased apart in lab today, the trapezius and latissimus dorsi. A flap of gray skin hangs from his side, cut unevenly, how a child with his first pair of scissors might do it. I'm still a novice with the scalpel.

When he finds the bottle of cheap brandy I use for cooking, he pours himself a glass. I add some salt to the pasta I'm boiling and tell myself to get more sleep. I promise to go to bed early tonight, close the textbooks by midnight. But he's still there, sipping the brandy.

"Should you really be drinking?" I ask.

"Why not? Doesn't really matter anymore," he says. He's facing me now, completely naked. In the lab, he was covered in a muslin sheet with frayed edges. It's hard not to look at his shriveled genitals.

"Didn't you die of liver failure?" I say.

"Maybe I did. No harm now, young lady."

"Fine. Just don't scare my mother. Wait," I say. "You didn't—you didn't come to take her, did you?"

"I'm no grim reaper, I'll tell you that. I'll be good."

I start the cream sauce and cook the shrimp. For my mother's birthday, I'm making her favorite meal. There's a cake too, but her day nurse bought it from the bakery section so I feel guilty. My mother used to be an excellent baker.

Gabe leans on the counter. He takes dainty sips of the brandy. I finish the shrimp Alfredo and, after a moment, divide it into two portions. I don't want to encourage him to stay.

In the dining room, my mother tries to light a candle, her hand trembling, the flame dancing. I take the lighter from her and light the tall candles with images of saints printed on the frosted glass holders, the cheap ones you find in the grocery store. A whole cluster of them. They fill the middle of the table like a fiery bouquet.

"There," she says, flipping the light switch off.

"I don't know if I can see my food."

"Then look," she says, "harder." She speaks softly, slurring the words together.

"Sit, Mom, it's your birthday," I say, serving her first. I overcooked the noodles to make them easier to swallow. She shuffles to her chair and I cut the fettuccine and shrimp into small pieces, making vertical and horizontal swipes, then diagonal cuts to get the last of it.

"That should do it," I say. "I used your recipe."

Gabe strolls in. He's poured himself another glass and joins us at the table. My mother doesn't react. She doesn't even see him. I wind a single noodle around my fork and twirl it until the noodle forms a little nest. Since my mother takes so long to eat, I have to make a game of this. I would've taken her to a nice restaurant, but she's too embarrassed to eat in public. People stare.

"You see patients today?" she asks, using as few words as possible. It's getting difficult for her to speak.

"No, not exactly. We won't see real patients for a few semesters."

"What did you do?"

"I had biochem and anatomy lab. We looked at the muscles of the back today."

Gabe smiles and takes a drink. His lips are pinkish gray and tight against his teeth.

"I may do that," my mother says, "donate my body." With her blank expression, another symptom of the disease, I can't tell if she's serious or not. So I change the subject.

"Do you like the shrimp?" I ask.

"It's lovely."

I twist another noodle around my fork. It's mushy and limp.

"Who is this one?" I say, pointing to the nearest saint candle. I hold it up for her to see.

"Saint Vitus. Protects against the shakes," she says. She pauses from the effort. "In the Middle Ages, the Saint Vitus Dance." She giggles. My mother doesn't laugh very often. She begins to cough, then gasp for air. I almost expect Gabe to take her away with him.

This isn't the first time this has happened. She calmly takes a sip of water, the liquid sloshing in the glass from her tremor, and swallows the food.

"Kate," she says. "No ventilator and no feeding tube. If it comes to that."

"Are you sure?"

"Yes. You understand? No tube."

"Fine," I say. My promise is hollow. I can't watch her die.

Gabe burps. He covers his mouth.

"Excuse me," he says.

• • •

In lab that day, we all donned crisp white lab coats and hovered around the stainless steel tables. The smell of embalming fluid made me a little dizzy. We would meet our cadavers soon.

My lab partners, Rachel and Ali, stood a few inches from the table. Rachel kept clasping her gloved hands together, rubbing the latex nervously. Ali reviewed our anatomy text, nodding his head a lot.

"Male, right?" he said, referring to our cadaver under the muslin sheet.

"I think so," I said. "He seems pretty flat—no breast bump."

"Should we uncover him?" Ali said.

"Sure," I said. "Rachel, are you ready for this?"

"Yes," she squeaked.

I peeled back the sheet. The body was positioned on its stomach, its back to us. It hardly looked human. White hairs sprouted from his fleshy back. The skin was greenish gray and wrinkled like old leather. Although his face was pressed against the table, I had to look at it. Eyes closed, lips slightly pursed. We were all relieved that he didn't have the death scream, mouth wide open, fighting for the last breath.

"That's one ugly bastard," Ali said.

We already knew his cause of death, liver failure, so he wasn't emaciated like the cancer bodies. I was pleased with his musculature. He would be an excellent specimen.

"Thank you," Rachel whispered to him.

"What?" Ali said.

"I was thanking him for his sacrifice. Thanking him for donating his body so we can learn. He's like an angel."

I'd memorized the lab instructions and watched the video at least four times, so I was getting impatient.

"We have to stick this block under his chest for support," I said. "You guys lift his head and shoulders and I'll position the block. On three?"

Ali grabbed the shoulders while Rachel gingerly touched his head.

"One . . . two . . . three."

His upper body was heavier than we'd expected. There was a large incision in his neck where his blood had been drained. Rachel dabbed it with a sponge, washing his body with Biostat as we'd been instructed to do. She smoothed the sponge along his entire body in careful strokes.

"Gabriel," she said. "We should call him Gabriel."

"How about Gabe?" Ali said.

"Gabe," I said. "Time to draw." I pulled out a purple marker and made a dotted line from the base of his head to the point of his buttocks. Then I made a horizontal line under the shoulder blades. Ali, eager to help, finished by drawing more horizontal lines, three inches wide, neat sections. This would help when we removed the skin.

"Can I cut first?" I asked. Ali handed me a scalpel.

I pointed the scalpel along the midline and thrust the blade into the skin. It was stiff and leathery. Rachel whispered, "I'm sorry, Gabe, I'm so sorry," over and over. I concentrated on the line I'd drawn, pulled the scalpel along the purple dots. I'm not sorry, Gabe. One of our instructors walked by, murmuring, "Good, good."

Next I plunged the blade into my horizontal dotted line. When I finished the cut, I pulled up a corner of skin with forceps. The subcutaneous fat was bright yellow, a vivid contrast to the gray skin. I kept pulling, slicing away the dense fat with my scalpel. In some places I could see the muscle underneath. Soon I had skinned a rectangular section of his back.

"Wow," Ali said.

Rachel looked as if she were in pain, her face red and scrunched up.

Ali wanted to cut. We finished skinning his back and be-

gan to scrape the fat from the trapezius and latissimus dorsi.
I pulled up a beautiful triangle of the trapezius with my forceps. Rachel wasn't so impressed.

"Do you want to hold the trapezius?" I asked. "It's so well defined."

"No, I'll just watch this time."

"I'm glad I don't eat meat," I said.

Rachel didn't laugh. I imagined Gabe using this muscle, rowing a canoe down the river, tossing his grandchild in the air, lifting a bag of groceries. But the thought was fleeting. If I considered him a person, I'd never make it through anatomy.

In our next lab, we take apart Gabe's spinal cord and I manage to get spinal fluid in my hair. When I return home, Gabe's sitting on the steps waiting for me.

"My back's killing me," he says.

"Funny," I say. "Were you a comedian?"

"No, just a retired teacher."

"Is that why you donated your body?"

"You're exactly right, young lady."

I hate this young lady crap. I step past him, glance at his dissected back. The spinal cord is fascinating and much thicker than I'd expected, considering it seems so delicate. I unlock the door, jiggling the key to make it fit. Maureen, my mother's health aide, is on the other side. She slings her purse over her ample chest.

"I'm sorry," I say, acknowledging my lateness.

"Have to pick up Emma," she says, slipping her feet into rubber clogs. "Bye now."

My mother sits on a chair in the middle of the living room, her face partially obscured by wet strips of plaster. It looks like a death mask but Maureen's left holes for her mouth and eyes.

My mother grabs another white strip and dunks it in the bowl of water to activate the plaster, but drops it on the floor. Gabe watches everything.

"Damn," she says.

"What exactly are you doing?"

"For a shrine in Brazil. People leave replicas of the diseased body part"—she pauses—"pray to the Virgin and wait for a miracle." She speaks without moving her jaw or the drying plaster.

"So you're doing your whole head?" I ask.

"Yes."

"Aw, let her have some fun," Gabe says. "While she still has hope."

"Hope is dangerous," I say.

My mother sighs, exhaling through her nose. One day last year, when the DMV took away her license, she gave up on science and medicine. She quit volunteering at the library and started wearing a gold cross around her neck. Just like that.

I notice the gray roots peeking through her scalp. When I have time, I'll touch them up with #54 Cinnamon Espresso. I smooth plastic wrap over my mother's hair to protect it from the plaster.

"You'll go with me? To Brazil?" she says.

"I have school, Mom. What did you eat today?"

"Oh, I don't remember."

"I'll make something quick. How about mac and cheese?"

"Lovely. Will be dry soon."

"Don't mind me," Gabe says. "I'm lactose intolerant."

I submerge a strip in the water, carefully adding it to the white mask. Later, I make macaroni from a box and unpack the overnight bag my mother left by the front door. I don't even know how she got it there by herself. While I'm studying at my desk, Gabe watches me from the window seat, smoking a cigarette. He's careful to blow the smoke out the window.

We're dissecting his forearm and hand when Rachel has a breakdown. She picks out the ripple of tendons with forceps and cleans them with a scalpel. I pull on the tendons to make his fingers curl.

"Cool," Ali says.

We tease apart the tendons for each finger. The forearm is an intricate network of muscle and tendon and bone.

"Check it out," Ali says, pulling on the middle tendon, the extensor digitorum. "He's giving us the finger."

Rachel stares for a moment, then snaps off her gloves and heads for the door.

"It was a joke, Rachel," Ali says.

"I'll go," I say. "Keep working on the hand."

I find Rachel in the locker room, lying on a bench. She's tracing the wood grain and trying not to cry.

"We didn't mean to be disrespectful," I say. "We need your help in there."

"You'll do just fine without me."

"You learn and recite each nerve and muscle before we even figure out how to pronounce them."

"I can't do this," she says. "I can't even distance myself from my first patient."

I've never thought of Gabe as a patient. He's a body we're taking apart, piece by piece, to examine form and structure. He has long yellow fingernails and a strong back. He follows me around the house.

Gabe is smoking on the porch swing. Since we peeled away the muscle and tendons of his right hand, he holds the cigarette with the bones of his thumb and forefinger. His palmaris

longus sticks out as he lifts the cigarette to his mouth. We forgot to trim it.

"Smoking will kill you," I say.

"Too late now," he says. "Better check on your mother."

When I enter the living room, the sharp smell of urine
greets me. I see her slumped in her easy chair, motionless. For
a moment, I think this may be the end. But when I face her, she
coughs, flings open her eyes. She's wearing her nightgown.

"Didn't Maureen help you get dressed today?" I ask.

"Fired," my mother replies. On her bad days, she uses single words to communicate.

"Why did you do that? She was really good. And I can't be
here all the time. You know that. I'm going to call her and
apologize."

"Bitch."

I don't know if she's talking about me or Maureen.

"Come on," I say. "Let's get you up."

Her arm jerks forward. I have a feeling she hasn't taken her
meds today, so there's more to come. Her legs twitch in a spas-
tic choreography.

"Wanna dance?" I say. We play this game when the drugs
wear off. I help her up. It's better to laugh than cry.

My mother's right leg shoots out. I mirror her movements,
clap my hands. Her left arm goes up, over her head, hand flail-
ing as if she were drowning. I copy her strange rhythm. We
dance.

"Faster," I say.

She wiggles her hips and smiles. Gabe joins us, shaking,
twisting, laughing.

We've cut apart Gabe's major muscles and limbs. Rachel has
returned. Ali and I act as though nothing happened, working
on his chest. After we reflect the skin, we cut his ribs with a

tool that looks like sharp pliers. I have to use two hands to
squeeze before the bone cracks. Squeeze, crack. I cut the right
side and Ali does the left. Then we lift the breastbone and ribs,
the whole thing hard and curved like a tortoiseshell. His deflated lungs are dark with tar.

"A smoker," Rachel says.

"Who still does that?" Ali says. "Europeans?"

"Maybe he's French," I say. "*Très romantique.*"

Rachel lifts one of the lungs and cuts the bronchus. She
points out a small white mass in the lung. One of the lab as-
sistants hovers over our group.

"Looks malignant," he says, drifting to the next table.

"I thought he died of liver failure," I say. I feel betrayed.
Gabe never mentioned this. We find several more tumors.

"Maybe his doctor screwed up," Rachel says. "It happens.
We're all human."

My mother refuses to get out of bed. I couldn't get her up that
morning, and I haven't hired another nurse yet. Tendrils of
her hair spread across the pillow like tentacles.

"Die," she says. "Die, die, die."

"Right," I say. "That would solve the problem." As I say it, I
realize it may be true. I am a terrible daughter. My father left
when he couldn't handle it anymore. They'd been on the brink
for years, separated several times, but her rapid deterioration
got to him. I think it was the adult diapers that finally did it.

Gabe watches us. He's looking worse for wear, his chest
wide open with one pitiful lung, one hand and foot stripped
to the bone, flaps of gray skin and muscle hanging from his
body.

"Let her do what she wants," he says. "You're not her
doctor."

"Mom," I say, stroking her hair, "where's that shrine in Brazil? Maybe we can go next summer. I'll call a travel agent."

"Too late," she says.

"Now you're being difficult. I know you want to go."

"No. *No.*"

"We could get great tans."

"Winter," she says. "Winter!"

"Southern hemisphere. You're right—it would be winter there, wouldn't it? But how cold does it get?"

She doesn't reply. Her arm jerks forward.

"Are you trying to punch me?" I say. "I can take a hint. You need to eat. Tomato soup okay?"

She nods. I go into the kitchen and Gabe follows.

"I have a bone to pick with you," I tell him.

"Haha," he says, lighting a cigarette. The smoke comes out his chest through the bronchus that Rachel severed.

"You didn't have hepatitis, did you? You had lung cancer." I twist the can opener, using too much force, tipping the can over.

"You saw it yourself. Why are you asking me?"

"I thought you died of liver failure."

"Ah, the great mystery," he says. He gets close and blows smoke in my face. I cough and tell him to get out of my kitchen.

"That's no way to talk to your teacher," he says.

We cut open the pericardium, the sac that protects the heart. We name the different chambers and structures that we can see, then use a blade to remove the heart from the chest. Gabe's heart. I hold it with both hands. To see inside, we have to cut it open. Ribbons of heart tissue cling to my scalpel.

• • •

My mother is gluing her plaster mask when I get home. The sides almost fit together, except for a gap at the top. It's eerie to see a replica of her head in white plaster. Gabe looks over my shoulder.

"Nice," he says.

"Salvador," my mother says. "Salvador, Brazil."

"I'll call a travel agent and see what we can do."

"You're learning," Gabe says.

I don't want to speak to him, not yet. His chest is nearly hollow. "So how's the new girl?" I ask my mother.

"Kelly," she says. "She's okay. I think she ate the pickles."

"Pickles. Weird."

"I'm basically a pickle, you know," Gabe says. "Preserved to last a long time."

"But otherwise Kelly's okay?" I ask. "She helped you bathe and make breakfast and lunch and everything? Did she take you to the library?"

"Yes," my mother says. "I got a Brazil guide."

"Good. That's good."

She holds up the plaster cast. Her fingers tremble as they always do. Suddenly everything seems real. Someday soon I will lose her. I go into the bathroom because I don't want her to see me like this.

In my head, I go over the structures of the cardiovascular system as I fight back tears. Gabe puts a bony hand on my shoulder.

"Jesus," I say. "You can't scare me like that."

"Have you figured it out?" he says.

"You did it to yourself. Because of your prognosis. You took something and poisoned your liver."

"You're the grand prize winner. I smoked for less than ten years. Quit when my daughter was born," he says.

"You didn't want to see yourself deteriorate, did you? Die slowly, in increments. That was your choice."

"Exactly," he says. "I didn't want my last glimpse to be of a hospital parking lot. They'd poke and prod and I'd get a nasty infection in my central line. I'd be on the vent, which would give me pneumonia. Finally I'd drown in my own lung fluid."

"You refused further medical intervention," I say, thinking out loud.

"Even if I survived for a few more months, I still had meta-static cancer. It's called quality of life," Gabe says. "Now let's have a drink while I still have a digestive system."

We take him apart, piece by piece. We cut open his stomach and see the remains of his last meal, which smells fishy and buttery like lobster. We take out his swollen liver, his spleen, his intestines, everything. We poke and slice his insides until there's hardly anything left.

When it's time to dissect the pelvis, we let Ali take over. Even he is out of jokes. Rachel flushes at the sight of the limp penis. I hold my breath. As Ali saws in a vertical line, from genitals to navel, he looks pained. Then he saws the abdomen from the torso. Gabe's legs are now detached, like a magi-cian's trick gone wrong. We're supposed to hemisect the pel-vis for a better view of the internal structures—bladder, pros-tate, testes.

That isn't the worst of it. Before our final two weeks of lab, our instructors prepare the cadavers' heads. They use an electric saw to cut the skull and face in half, down the midline. Gabe is reduced to the left half of his head. We lift the muslin shroud. On the side of his chin, there's a small scar I've never noticed. On the bridge of his nose, a few dark freckles. We flip him over. Inside, everything is pinkish gray, grayish pink. Part of his tongue, his teeth, his sinuses, his brain. He's missing two molars.

We take out the left hemisphere of his brain, the side associated with logic and reason. It's not exactly true—the neural circuitry isn't that simple. I hold Gabe's brain in my hands, trace my fingers along the wrinkled fissures. I wonder what memories are locked deep inside. I commit the structures to memory: central sulcus, lateral sulcus, cingulate sulcus.

For my mother and me, it won't be easy. But sometimes, sometimes, we'll dance.

When a Camel Breaks Your Heart

YOUR LOVER HASN'T always been a camel. Yesterday Mahir was human, painfully human, a stubborn medical student who wanted to save the world. Peek into the living room to see if the camel's still there. Affirmative. He takes up the entire futon, legs folded neatly under him, and his hump towers over the room.

The image reminds you of a Magritte painting: *Ceci n'est pas une pipe.* This is not a pipe. What you see and what you know aren't the same. You know it's Mahir, but you see a camel. You've only seen them in zoos, maybe a circus when you were a kid, but the identification is automatic—large humped mammal, with coarse hair the color of desert sand, equals camel. If you hadn't gagged on your coffee when you first saw him, you'd think you were in a crappy dream. But you tasted the sour stomach acid mixed with the bitter Sumatra blend, so by then several senses had confirmed the new reality. *This is not a human.*

An inside joke made manifest. Your boyfriend, the traitor, taking the easy way out—this way, all the messy breaking done for him—Mahir's human form just disappears. Neat and tidy. If it were a bone breaking instead of a relationship, he'd call it a simple displaced fracture, in his medical parlance. Feel your insides twist and ache from the emptiness. First Mahir betrays you, then your own stomach. Your eyes still perceive a camel. Maybe you'll try reasoning with him. The camel intently watches the war on television, everything in eerie green because it's night over there. It's the American invasion, round two.

The futon, which you'd always meant to replace with a real sofa after college, sags under his weight. The other accoutrements of two graduate students—the overburdened IKEA bookshelves, the record player and vinyl collection with every Kinks album produced, along with the coffee table made of stacked shipping pallets—appear untouched.

Are camels violent? you wonder. Lace up your tennis shoes in case you have to run. But acknowledge the animal even smells like Mahir, of laundry soap and citrus shampoo. He's weeping, the poor beast is weeping. You didn't know such emotion was possible from an animal.

"Oh, sweetheart," you say. "Please don't cry."

His eyes are dark and glossy. A tear rolls down the fur on his cheek, landing on the red futon. Touch his soft, velvety nose. The tactile sensation surprises you.

On the television, watch the circles of light grow and radiate outward from a small flash in the sky. Some of them expand to fill the screen with pale green light. They fade quickly and shadow engulfs the view. Consider how you would draw the scene. There is light and dark with no intermediate shades, fire against night air. But the energy is kinetic—it can't be held captive on paper. A two-dimensional rendering won't suffice. And this is no time for art.

"There's nothing we can do," you say aloud. "Why don't

we watch something else? Maybe"—here you giggle nervously—"the nature channel? Or Animal Planet?"

Recognize that he doesn't find your joke funny because his focus never wavers. Another flash in the green sky, another circle of light. The bombs are more regular now, as if they're controlled by a timer. On television, they never hit anything—they simply fly in the air and explode like fireworks. For you, it's easier to appreciate their beauty than to think about what's really happening.

"Mahir," you say. "It's okay, baby."

He shakes his head no and makes a grunting noise as if trying to speak. Several short grunts, in fact, that mean nothing to you.

"I don't understand, baby." Take a tissue and dab the water from his eyes. It's a steady stream. Still, he watches the bombing. The fur on his cheeks is matted from the path of tears.

"I'll get you some water," you say. When you were a little girl, your mother always made you drink a glass of water when you were crying. It was impossible to drink the water and cry at the same time. Welcome the task—anything to keep your hands busy and mind occupied.

Fill a large bowl with tap water and place it by the sofa. Of course he won't drink—those black eyes remain locked on the television.

"No water?" you ask. "It will make you feel better. How about some food? Are you hungry?"

He shakes his head again, his teeth grinding. The weeping continues unabated, despite your efforts. The futon mattress absorbs the tears.

Why a camel of all creatures? you think. You'd discussed getting a pet together, but dogs weren't considered clean animals in Mahir's faith. You talked about choosing a cat from the shelter, but last night Mahir announced that he wanted a camel and you played along with the joke. You thought it was a nod to the stereotypes but also a fantasy that you two could get an exotic animal and make everything work. Now you don't know anything. Camel trumps reason.

"Is this a protest?" you say. "That's what it is, isn't it? How is it a protest if I'm the only one who knows?" Performance art with an audience of one. Frustration simmers in your chest and threatens to bubble into anger. Admit this is getting ridiculous.

He swings his head toward you and blinks, one eye faster than the other.

"Snap out of it, okay?" you say. "You haven't eaten anything all morning. You're probably starving."

Focus on the new task, but realize that you have no idea what camels eat. Consider ordering Mahir's favorite cheese pizza from Bella Italia. When you fasted with him last Ramadan, you got plain pizza frequently. He timed it carefully so the delivery guy would arrive at sunset, moments after you'd broken your fasts with a quick kiss and Mahir had bowed his head to the ground. You were fascinated by the process. But you lasted only a week. A week! To think you'd considered converting to Islam, even though you're a dedicated agnostic—you admit there could be something greater than ourselves, but none of the organized religions has it right. Yet you were willing to forgo your own fundamental beliefs and adopt his, if that's what it took. You'd even stayed around for the grad program, even though the art school isn't top notch, because Mahir got into the first-rate medical school here.

During that week of fasting, Mahir explained that his parents might not accept you even if you became Muslim. He said you were still an outsider because you were American and white. His parents wouldn't care that he was a successful doctor if he married outside the community.

Considering the situation, shouldn't you be the one who's crying? Open the pantry in search of camel food. The shelves are bare—you were going to buy groceries today. There's a can of tomato soup, a half-eaten package of dates, and a bottle of pinot noir you were saving for a special occasion. Let the pantry door slam shut. The refrigerator is just as barren, only some pita bread and strawberry jam.

"How about toasted pita and jam? Or pizza?" you call from the kitchen. When you don't receive an answer, you return to the living room, stepping in a pile of camel dung. Feel both disgusted and heartbroken by the manure squishing between your toes. Consider it a metaphor for your relationship.

"No more!" you say, turning off the television. "You are not allowed to watch anymore. And you can stop the protest. I get it."

The weeping is now sobbing, complete with heaves and sniffles. A sad camel. You wonder if they really can store water in their humps.

Remember the good times, when Mahir was still human. For example, when you first moved into the apartment together. The previous tenant had shut off the electricity, so the two of you ate Thai takeout by candlelight, sitting Indian style on the wood floor in front of a makeshift table made of stacked textbooks. Neither of you had much of an appetite—too giddy from sharing the same space. Or the time you drove Mahir's car to Miami on a whim, because neither of you had seen dolphins in the Atlantic and there were still four days until spring semester began, so why not? And the time last year when you were sick with strep, feeling razor blades every time you swallowed, but Mahir took excellent care of you, at your side with chicken broth and a cool washrag, for days. In between fever dreams, you decided that you really, truly loved this boy.

Now remember the not-so-good times too. Like when his parents came to visit for a weekend and you had to stay with your friend Eva, but not before erasing all traces of your existence from the apartment. You had to take all of your drawings and supplies to your studio on campus, put your clothes and shoes in boxes and stuff them in the closet, and keep your toothbrush and mascara and vanilla lotion in your purse. Even the kitchen was a potential landmine—you had to hide your coffeemaker (Mahir hates coffee) and Nutella (ditto anything hazelnut), among other things. In contrast, when your parents visited, they were worried they'd make some kind of faux pas in front of Mahir (no pork or shellfish, you told them), but their concerns evaporated once they got to know him. They were just glad to see you happy.

Don't forget the time Mahir took you to the artisan jewelers to pick out a necklace for your birthday, and when you walked in, the salesgirl stood beaming behind the display of engagement rings. The flicker of hope burned bright, so close you could feel the heat on your fingertips, but only for a moment before Mahir said, "Oh, no, we'd like to see the necklaces." You managed to leave the store before you had the meltdown, saving the snot-faced sobbing for the car. Mahir, trying to smooth things over, said they don't do rings in his culture anyway, which only increased the waterworks.

Most of all, remember what happened last night. You were taking a bath, scrubbing the cuff of brown dots and arabesques you'd painted on your left ankle. But it refused to fade. You could feel the pulse there, just under the bone: *thump, thump.*

"'Heart?'" Mahir said from the hallway.

"In here." Annoyed by the way he shortened the word "sweetheart," you slipped your leg into the bathwater to hide the henna. In his culture, women decorated the bride's body with henna before the wedding. You knew it was foolish to practice on yourself but couldn't stop entertaining the fantasy of yourself as a hennaed bride. After three years together, the fantasy didn't seem so far-fetched.

Mahir leaned in the doorway, his arms crossed, but smiling at the discovery of your nakedness.

"Ah, just what I wanted," he said.

"Don't you always, M?"

Mahir knelt by the tub. He gently lifted your right leg, the one without the henna, exposing its full length to the air. Holding it up with one hand, his other hand circled your thigh. You closed your eyes to savor the sensation—you'd been waiting for this. The cold air crept up your leg.

"Let's see," he said. He brushed the top of your thigh with a long index finger. "Sartorius, rectus femoris."

Oh, right—he wanted to study your anatomy, in the literal sense. He moved his finger toward your knee. The moment ruined, your heartbeat slowed to its normal rate and you opened your eyes.

"Vastus lateralis, vastus medialis," he said.

His every thought related to medical school. He was always in his own head. Even when he wasn't studying, he would go running for miles and miles just so he could think. Was he ever thinking about you?

Mahir's finger returned to your thigh and pointed to its underside.

"You should know this," you said.

His finger remained there, stumped.

"Biceps . . ." you started.

"Don't tell me. Femoris. Biceps femoris."

"Correct," you said. "You have permission to kiss my feet in gratitude."

"I am so very, very grateful," he said. He grabbed your right foot and, instead of kissing your big toe, he bit down.

"Hey!"

You were surprised that he didn't remember all the muscles you'd learned as undergrads, especially with all the repetition. As a budding artist, you'd taken the anatomy class to render the human form with greater accuracy. That first day in lecture, Mahir had sat directly in front of you, taking notes with a black Bic pen in neat, evenly spaced capital letters. The next class, you sat one seat over from him and studied the angle of his jaw in profile, his brown skin, his curly black hair. The following lecture, he asked you to study with him for the first exam, if you wanted, if you were free. You were attracted to the hesitant boy with two days' stubble on his chin, who wanted to work for Doctors Without Borders. He was dark and exotic and you wanted to make him pose for you.

Now you were an accomplished figure artist, working toward a graduate degree. You had your own students and you urged them to take anatomy courses. How could they draw the human body without knowing what was inside?

In the bathtub, you suddenly felt the urge to draw Mahir again, another portrait to join the other charcoal sketches scotch-taped to the ceiling of your shared bedroom. Instead you fingered the V-shaped collar of his cotton shirt.

"Why don't you join me?" you said.

"I'm studying."

"Just anatomy?"

"And biochem and ethics."

"Is that all? Those aren't very important," you said. But you knew he was lying—studying was just a cover. He looked upward, his eyes bloodshot from fatigue.

"What's wrong?" you said.

"I should be there," Mahir said, referring to the war. "I could help triage or something."

"Is it worth leaving the people you love, the people right

in front of you?" you asked. He didn't see you. For a budding doctor with empathy to spare, he couldn't recognize the injuries he'd caused you, or even your state of mind. Still, you tried to understand his perspective.

"Why don't we gather basic supplies for the civilians?" you continued. "You know, bottled water, nonperishables, some clothing?"

"Maybe."

He'd refused to read the newspapers for the past two weeks. But he was still lured by the television, sucked in by the moving images. Me, you remember thinking, I am here. Help me instead of strangers.

The war was over there, far from you and Mahir. But it wasn't too far from the homeland of his parents, just a couple of countries away, a place that you couldn't pronounce correctly. Whenever you tried, Mahir made fun of you. He said you pronounced it like the American journalists.

You sat up in the tub. You pulled off his shirt and he didn't resist. Then he turned to leave, revealing his brown back. The muscle dipped and formed a valley in the center, along the narrow column of his spine. The light followed a path inward from each side of his back—it became lost in the valley. This was where you would leave a long black smudge of charcoal on the paper.

"Please come in?"

"I can't, hon," he said.

You sank into the water, submerged your head and waited. Nearly a minute passed before you came up for air, because you were mostly joking. You wondered if he would recognize the desperation. Probably not, given his mental state.

"Did you think that would work?" he said.

"Maybe."

"You're always right, aren't you?"

You laughed. As he took off his jeans and stepped into the tub, the water level rose. He struggled to find a comfortable position facing you. You twisted your torso and rested your weight on one hip. Two bodies didn't fit in the old clawfoot tub, at least not the two of you.

"Mahir!" you protest. "That hurts!"

"What, 'heart?"

"You're on my *foot*." You wondered how he could be so blind to your needs, even the physical ones.

Finally, he shifted.

"Other one."

"Better?" he said.

"Yes." You propped one heel on his shoulder. You almost wanted him to see the henna you'd drawn, your efforts to understand.

"Did I hear the phone ring earlier?" you said.

"Your mother called."

"What did she want?"

"I don't know. You know, you really look more and more like her," he said.

"My mom? She's blond!" you said, indignant. You've always been a brunette. The better to match Mahir's dark features.

"I think your nose is getting pointy like hers," Mahir said. It was true. You'd examined your nose last week and attempted to draw a self-portrait. It was clearly your mother's nose.

"You look like your mother. Or maybe your father. But I wouldn't know, would I?" Your words hung in the air like steam from the bathwater.

"Please."

"Please what?" you said. You found it ironic that he spoke three languages but couldn't adequately express himself.

"Please. I love you." He reached for your hand; you pulled it away.

"Do you? Prove it."

"What do you want from me?"

"I want to have dinner with your parents," you said. You wanted to dine with them in an ethnic restaurant and eat foods rich in flavorful spices. And you wanted to know if Mahir's mother would wear a headscarf and robe or a shirt and trousers. Really, though, you wanted your future to include Mahir, and he was making it clear this was not an option.

"Do you have to do this now?" Mahir's eyes were full and glossy. You felt a fleeting sense of satisfaction.

"Why not now? When?" you said, splashing water in his face, but he didn't even blink.

"The world is a mess. People will die," he said.

"When will you decide?" you yelled. You struggled to understand his simple fate: he was first-generation North American and his parents expected him to find a nice Muslim girl. But it was more likely that they would find her first. Mahir was now of marrying age.

If he chose you, his parents might disown him. Or they might not. Mahir couldn't bring himself to tell them yet, he said he wasn't ready to break their hearts. Sometimes, when you lay awake, you thought him a coward.

He didn't talk much about his parents or their homeland. He had been there a few times, the last nearly three years ago, just before he met you. But it was there, in him, always—in his skin, his faith, everything.

"They're going to do it," he said.

"Your parents?"

"The government. America," he said. "Us." He was referring to the bombing campaign.

"You weren't studying," you said. Mahir rose and the water level returned to the top of your breast. He left the room without a towel, naked and dripping water on the tile.

You let him cool off for a while. When you finally got out of the tub, you slipped into his white terrycloth robe. Of course, you found him in the living room, watching the live news coverage, hunched forward on the futon, chewing on his thumbnail.

You studied the high forehead, deep-set eyes, and dark hair of a Muslim man being interviewed on TV, your eyes straining to read the captions. When you couldn't stand to see anymore, you turned it off. Wedging yourself between the futon and his back, you tucked your ankle under the robe. You wrapped your body around his. Inhale, exhale. Together, your lungs expanded and chests rose. Then your lungs deflated and chests fell. The rhythm felt good.

"What can I do?" you said.

"Let's get a camel. You know, instead of a cat."

"Where do you get a camel?" you said, smiling.

"I don't know. I rode one once, when I was visiting my grandparents. We definitely need an authentic one," he said. Your ear was pressed against his back and you felt the vibrations from his voice.

"An import?"

"Yeah, we need to naturalize one."

"One hump or two?" You kissed the birthmark on his shoulder, a drop of ink marring an otherwise clean canvas.

"One, I think."

"Why just one?" You could play this game, maybe even believe it.

"They're better for riding. And they can store more water in one big hump. What should we name it?" he said.

"Hmm . . . how about Shiraz?" you suggested. Shiraz the camel sounded about right.

"No, Zamboni."

"Zamboni?"

"Zamboni," Mahir repeated, with that satisfied tone he got when he knew he was right.

"Okay," you said. You pictured the large machine that smoothed ice, rolling over the rough patches to produce a slick, uniform surface. But you knew that Mahir chose the name because, to his ear, it sounded whimsical and more American.

"I know, babe, I know," you said.

"You don't. But you try."

You hesitated. "Is that enough for you?" Because that was all you had to give.

"Yes," he said. "It has to be. What will we feed Zamboni?"

"I don't know." You shrugged. "What do camels eat?"

"Hay maybe?"

"Does hay grow there?"

"I don't know, 'heart."

Suddenly, you had the urge to make love, because halfway around the world, people like Mahir were dying. You kept your eyes open to remember his fleshy earlobes, the small scar at the base of his chin, the irises so dark they melted into his pupils. You were unsure how much longer you could wait, or if he would ever decide.

By afternoon, Mahir the camel has more of a musky, animal smell. He stinks.

"You can end the protest now. It's not very effective." Wonder if he might be protesting *you* rather than the war. Or your relative indifference to the invasion. Despite your weak stomach, pour yourself a second glass of the pinot noir. Enjoy the warmth tingling through your body. The camel now appears to be nibbling on the futon.

You're not prepared to let go, not today. Maybe you will keep him as a pet for a while. Somewhere, you'll find alfalfa hay if that's what he eats, and you'll measure his food every morning and night. You'll set up a pen in the living room. The zoo—of course—you will go to the zoo and observe the camels. Maybe interview the zookeeper who takes care of them.

You've already bought cat litter to clean up the dung. Straw for his bedding will be harder to find. Where can you buy straw this time of year?

"Mahir?" you say. "Just come back. Please. Whatever you want me to do, I'll do it."

Suddenly, ponder your own culpability in this mess. Have you forced him to such extreme measures? Should you be happy living in the moment, no concern for a future with Mahir? Can you ever understand him? Maybe if you play along, act normal, he'll become human again.

He stopped crying at least an hour ago, but he doesn't look at you.

"Zamboni?"

Upon hearing his name, the camel swings his head toward you. His nostrils flare as he exhales.

"Pose for me," you say. Not that he's moving much anyway. Pull out a sketch pad and charcoal, then sit across from him. Forming the shapes first, the underlying structure, is difficult. This body is unfamiliar. A cylinder, no, an oval for the main part. Then there is the question of the hump. Should you add a half sphere on top?

The sketch looks like a cross between a horse and a llama. Be frustrated that you can't draw a goddamned camel. So abandon your sketch and try to sit with him, squeezing onto the futon. Stroke his nose, and Zamboni will nuzzle you in return. He swings a cloven foot onto your lap. Yelp in pain.

"You're hurting me," you say. "It hurts!"

He licks your face before you can get up. Your cheek feels hot and itchy, as if you're having an allergic reaction. Zamboni tries to follow you, planting his forelegs on the floor and pushing off from his back legs, like an old man using a cane to get up, maximizing leverage, until all four legs touch the ground. He rises to his full height, but not without hitting his head and scraping his hump on the ceiling. You're afraid he'll touch you again, so climb in the bay window frame and balance there. Say a secular prayer for whoever invented bay windows.

"Look, I'm trying," you say from your temporary haven. "I know you feel helpless. But I don't know what to do."

Zamboni chews on the hem of your jeans. Old jeans, sure, but you'd like to keep them intact.

"Hey, stop it." Pull your leg away but realize he has a tight grip. "Seriously. Knock it off."

He's ripped a patch of denim and seems to be eating it. His jaws have a firm grasp of your entire pants leg. Be alarmed. Wriggle from the jeans, taking care not to lose your balance. Zamboni continues to chew with your jeans hanging from his mouth. You're left in just your underwear.

"I offered food earlier," you say. "Now you're hungry? What more do you want?"

When you try to make your escape, he lunges for your hair and grabs a mouthful. Scream. Then rip out some hair for him, shouting, "Take it, just take it." Manage to lock yourself in the bedroom.

This is ridiculous, you think, the camel is no longer Mahir. You couldn't possibly keep him, and you'd known that all along. Open the bedroom door, just a crack, to see what he's doing. He's staring out the window, looking at nothing, being a camel. Feel a wave of grief but refuse to cry. Instead, open the phone book to find animal control.

"Hi," you say into the phone, the landline you share with Mahir, "do you handle large animals?"

"Yes, ma'am."

"You're not going to believe this," you say. Wonder if he'll think you're crazy. Who cares at this point?

"We've seen just about everything, ma'am."

"There's a camel in my apartment."

"Bactrian or dromedary?" says the voice, flat as fresh asphalt. No need to worry about this guy's judgment.

"Excuse me?" you say, to be sure you heard him correctly.

"Does he have one hump or two? That's how we classify them."

"One," you say. Give the man your name and address. He says they'll be over soon. In the meantime, peek into the living room.

"Mahir," you say, "don't do this. Okay?"

Zamboni, apparently tired of ducking, has sunk back to the floor, his legs tucked under his massive body. No longer transfixed by what's outside the window, he bites the window frame, scraping the varnish with his teeth.

"Fine," you say. Enough.

Someone pounds on the front door. Zamboni is occupied with chewing the wood, so you sail to the door in a bathrobe and let two officers come in. They wear khaki uniforms with rolled-up sleeves.

"Did you call in a complaint, ma'am?" says the taller one.

"Yes," you say, pointing at Zamboni, who chews contentedly, moving his jaw in a rhythmic motion.

"Can you tell us what happened?" the tall officer says. The other one remains silent. He must be the muscle, you think.

"I don't know. He just appeared."

The officer looks skeptical. "So he's not your camel? Maybe he belongs to a neighbor? Somebody who wanted a party gag?"

Hesitate. "No," you say, "no, he's not mine." He never really was.

"When will people learn?" the tall officer says to no one in particular. "You just can't keep an exotic in an apartment."

"Right," you say.

"We'll get him out of here then. We have some paperwork for you to fill out."

Write the information without really seeing. It's more of an automatic response. Everything is happening so quickly. Sign your name as a big hollow loop.

"What will happen to him?" you ask.

"Oh, he'll probably go to the zoo or, if he's friendly, maybe a petting zoo for exotics." They have their hands all over him, prodding him with their fingers. They've secured his head with a rope halter. Despite the nudging, Zamboni doesn't budge and they try a new tactic.

"Hup," they say, making clicking noises. The tall officer pulls the rope at his head while the muscle officer pushes from behind, groaning.

Zamboni's front half is pulled forward. He opens his mouth and spits on the tall officer, nailing him right in the face. You can't help but laugh at the bravado. Part of you wants Zamboni to win this battle.

The officer wipes his face with his hand. "I've had worse," he says. "Just part of the job, I guess."

Nod in agreement. The muscle officer plants his feet, heaving forward, throwing his upper body into Zamboni. Thrown off balance, the camel struggles to his feet and takes a crouching step forward. Then they're leading him toward the door and you're trying not to cry.

"Sorry for the inconvenience, ma'am," says the tall officer. "Have a good day."

The hall ceiling, nearly two feet higher, allows Zamboni to reach his full height. His hump sways from side to side and his little tail swishes. Close the door, unable to decide if you feel remorse or relief.

Several days later, there's a tentative knock on the door. Mahir. Your heart jumps, does somersaults, a whole gymnastic routine in your chest. But through the peephole, you see a blur of skin the color of coffee ice cream, shoulder-length black hair.

Open the door to find his mother. Notice she's wearing dark jeans and a lamb's wool sweater. A brown Coach purse. Remember to breathe.

"Is Mahir here?" she asks in a singsong accent.

Say no.

"Have you seen him?"

Notice how a few strands of dark hair shine red in the hall light.

"I haven't seen him in days," you say truthfully.

"But you are—you are the girlfriend?"

You have no idea how to answer this question. Don't even try. Linger on her impersonal usage—the girlfriend. Not *his* girlfriend. Keep the tears at bay until she leaves by thinking about how much art you've produced in the last week. Maybe grief enhances your creativity.

"The medical school said he hasn't been in his classes," his mother says. "We are so worried."

"I'm sorry," you say, "but he hasn't contacted me."

"Can I see his room?" she asks. This is the question that cleaves your broken heart into pieces, because she knew all along. Mahir rejected you, wholly and completely, for who you are. You were his fling before settling down. He was your exotic, and you were his.

"He doesn't live here anymore," you say while biting the inside of your cheek.

Then, when you've locked the door, turn and keep your shoulders braced. Slide down the length of the door, feel the ground. Now try to cry. Better yet, figure out how to incorporate the last ninety-six hours into the narrative of your life.

Every month, go to the zoo to look for him. Linger at the camel pen. Camels are well liked—they're not as popular as the tigers, but people always bypass the marmosets to get to the camels. The zoo keeps the Bactrian and dromedary camels in the same area, a pen with sandy earth and spiky grass and fake rocks.

Someday you'll bring your sketchbook and try again. For now, bring newspaper clippings with updates on the war, tucking them in the chain-link fence. When nobody's around, whisper his name.

You can't distinguish him from the other camels. They stand, chewing on wisps of hay. Maybe they're hiding him, protecting one of their own. Wonder if you'll ever find him, and when you do, if he would even recognize you.

No Monsters Here

Hᴀɴɴᴀʜ ꜰᴏᴜɴᴅ ʜɪꜱ left ear in the laundry hamper. It was unmistakably her husband's—small with a leaf-shaped brown mole on the lobe. She ran to the television and turned it on, fearing the worst: a helicopter shot down. A mortar attack. A roadside bomb.

What had she done wrong? Ever since Hannah had been on the Sertraline, she'd lost the constant worries about her loved ones. Which was why she stopped taking the medication, to keep her family safe. That morning, Hannah had resumed her ritual of going through the family photo album and touching the middle of each picture of their daughter, always with her index finger, and wiping away the fingerprint with a paper towel. If she didn't get the exact middle of the photograph, Hannah would touch it again until she got it right—otherwise Lily would've drowned during Red Cross swimming lessons. Of course Hannah understood how ridiculous this sounded, but she'd been performing these behaviors for years and, as a result, nothing bad had ever happened.

Her therapist had been helping Hannah see that her anxieties were unfounded: she was instructed to think of something minor and specific, something that wouldn't be terrible if it *did* actually happen. For example, that morning, Hannah had been listening to NPR with headphones so she wouldn't wake Lily. She started tapping the left headphone as the sound cut out, and Hannah knew she had to tap the foam sixteen times or John would lose the hearing in his left ear. As directed by her therapist, she refused to perform the sequence, touching the headphone only once. Hearing loss on one side, while inconvenient, wouldn't be so terrible for him. But finding his ear in the laundry hamper amplified Hannah's worst nightmares.

Come back in one piece, she'd told him. In his civilian life, John had been a botanist who talked to his plants. *Hello, Violet. You're looking lovely today, Miss Sage.* He'd joined the National Guard expecting to help in mass casualties or natural disasters. But now he cared for soldiers in a field hospital halfway around the world. Still, he was an idealist. Hannah tried to picture him without an ear, just a hole on the left side of his head. Maybe he'd come home missing a leg or an arm. That she could probably deal with—something she could make a plan for: schedule the physical therapy appointments, research the best artificial limbs, install safety railings in the bathroom.

There was nothing on the evening news. Hannah waited for a compulsion to become clear, a sequence that would keep John safe. Maybe some of the Sertraline was still in her system, keeping the behaviors at bay. Her fingers ached from clutching the ear, all cold and fleshy like a dried apricot. Hannah resisted the urge to call the other wives—they would either make her hysterical with their speculation or tell her to toughen up and be strong. Instead she tucked the ear into her bra, close to her heart, and shivered. She didn't like the asymmetry.

On the kitchen counter, the indicator light on the laptop

glowed like a lightning bug, beckoning Hannah. She checked her e-mail, their main source of communication, hoping for a new message. Only old ones, the last few so brief and disjointed:

> *119 in the shade. took care of some iraqi kids. hope you*
> *understand why i'm doing this.*
> *bearhugs, j.*

And another, from the previous week:

> *very hot. icecream maker a big hit, great care*
> *package. love to my girls. j.*

The lack of capital letters, along with the odd number, 119, made Hannah straighten on the barstool, as if avoiding some invisible discomfort. She refreshed her e-mail four times and left the screen on, just in case. She waited for a phone call, some small reassurance, any information about her husband that would explain the seed of dread sprouting in the pit of her stomach.

Pulling the ear from her bra, Hannah wondered if her obsessive-compulsive tendencies were triggering delusions. As she watched CNN, she turned the ear in her palm, over and over, feeling the stiff cartilage. The edge that would attach to his head was smooth and clean, as if made of clay. In her mind, she replayed what she'd tell their six-year-old daughter.

Hannah chose their bedtime book carefully—a story about a young witch. Her father was a wizard who turned himself into a fox and couldn't teach her anymore. The young witch was just an apprentice, not yet a true witch, and after she lost her father, she kept messing up the spells.

"Mom," Lily said, "when will Daddy be home?"

"I don't know," Hannah replied. "What he's doing is very dangerous."

According to John's regular e-mails, missives that spanned several pages, this was not exactly true. Hannah didn't know what to believe. She knew, with certainty, that he was a medic in the reserves. He said when they got bored, they'd neuter the stray cats. There were hundreds of cats slinking around the compound. They'd grab a tomcat, put him under, and snip, snip. But she also knew that John didn't want her to worry, and he had a grand imagination. If the cats were a cover story, she'd never forgive him. She hated not knowing. How could she keep him from harm without more information? Her obsessions needed those specifics.

She smoothed the hair on her daughter's head. How could she possibly break this little heart? John couldn't go and die on them—he was the very person who kept Hannah in balance, the calm to her panic, the yin to her yang. He's the one who suggested that most people didn't have such ruminations and that she didn't have to live with them if she didn't want to. He also encouraged her to take the 100 milligrams of Sertraline every day.

"I know he loves us very much. No matter what," Hannah said to her daughter, trying to sound confident.

"Okay," Lily said. "Monster check."

Hannah opened the closet door: no monsters there. No monsters under the desk. But when Hannah checked under the bed, she was horrified to find her husband's right arm, nestled between two oblong boxes full of winter clothing, the fingers splayed as if reaching for something. Oh God, what did this mean? Leaving the arm in the shadows, she popped up and kissed Lily on the forehead, vowing not to worry her child.

"No monsters under the bed. You're all set. Good night, sweetie."

"Good night, Mom," Lily said.

Hannah clicked off the light. Had the medication suppressed her intuition, making her forget to do something to keep his right arm intact? Was she supposed to fold all of his shirts so the right sleeve was on top? Or reset the time on his chronograph watch, which he normally wore on his right arm but now sat on his dresser? Of course not. She was being irrational again. A spike, in therapy terms. Hannah pulled the index card from the bottom of her purse. In her own handwriting—neat capital letters—she'd written the words dictated by her therapist:

> MAYBE THIS AWFUL THING WILL HAPPEN. I
> WILL LIVE WITH THE POSSIBILITY AND TAKE
> THAT RISK.

Maybe John was gone forever. She would live with it and accept the risk, because that was her burden to bear for not saving him. Still, Hannah watched CNN for the next hour, seeing a report on women entrepreneurs and a segment on a courageous two-legged dog. No news of the war. How could John hold her with only one arm? When she was sure Lily was asleep, she crept into her daughter's room to retrieve the arm.

In the master bedroom, she studied the arm. It smelled faintly of sweat. The skin was pink, as if he'd been in the sun too long. White flakes of skin settled on the sun-bleached hairs, which grew in neat rows like grain. Before she went to bed, Hannah tucked the arm into the sheets and put the ear on his pillow and whispered, "Good night, good night."

• • •

Hannah couldn't sleep. She put the ear in the breast pocket of her jersey sleep shirt and wandered to the kitchen. She had one of John's goofy songs in her head, the one about Lily and their old cat:

> *Lily, Lily is so pretty,*
> *a beauty of a girl,*
> *with Romeo her magic cat*
> *they'll conquer the whole world.*

Hannah was a planner, and being a widow wasn't in her plans. She'd encountered slight deviations before—she planned to be a stay-at-home mom when Lily was born, and she had been, until a couple of years ago, when her sewing talent and word of mouth resulted in her own tailoring business. Her other plans had been fulfilled: get a teaching degree, teach for four years, be married by the time she was twenty-six. Have her first child by age twenty-eight, preferably a girl. While the modest tailoring business was unexpected, it fit neatly into the scheme of things, because Lily had been going to all-day kindergarten and Hannah could work from home.

Hannah loved the exact nature of sewing. Follow the pattern, and you'll have a lovely set of curtains for the living room. If you follow the plan, everything turns out right, and that's precisely what Hannah intended to do. Except she had no plan for a missing husband. If she had a corpse, at least she could put it in a casket and bury it in the ground along with her heart. With a body, with that certainty of knowledge, she could follow the stages of grief to the letter, take on the role of widow. Starting with denial (check that from the list), moving to anger, then—what came next? It didn't matter. Hannah would identify the remaining stages and complete them, just as other people did in a time of loss. And she'd be much more careful, for Lily's sake, performing whatever compulsions necessary.

She found herself in the basement, staring at the canned vegetables from last year's harvest. Why had she come down here? There must've been a reason, but Hannah couldn't remember. She felt a sense of calm among the neat rows of Mason jars. After checking to make sure each jar faced forward, she began to dust them with a paper towel.

Every year, John spent hours in the dirt. He grew bushels of vegetables. The tomatoes, peppers, and squashes covered every surface of the deck and attracted raccoons. Hannah preferred the relative order of the kitchen, where she chopped, stewed, and canned them for future use. Like much of their relationship, she made order from his chaos. And they made a good parenting team: John fun and spontaneous, Hannah organized and deliberate—an ideal balance.

The jars of tomatoes glowed red. On the next shelf, she dusted the military-green pickles and watched the sprigs of dill float leisurely in the vinegar. Below the pickles sat the jalapeño peppers he enjoyed so much. They were too spicy for Hannah. John ate them diced by the spoonful, sliced on burgers or sandwiches, sometimes whole dipped in melted Monterey Jack. She'd sent several jars in the latest care package.

On the bottom shelves she kept the emergency supplies: gallon jugs of water, an LED lantern with two extra packs of AA batteries, a wind-up radio, a big Rubbermaid tub of MREs (meals ready to eat). Four space foil blankets, folded in perfect squares. A flashlight that generated electricity when you shook it. A box of first aid supplies. A pack of playing cards. A sewing kit. None of these items would help in this emergency.

Hannah plopped down on the cot John kept in the corner.

She had only prepared for a certain type of emergency, not this kind of apocalypse, the end of her domestic world.

By the next morning, Hannah had found his other arm behind the computer monitor, his pelvis under the sofa cushions, his right leg in the broom closet, his right ear in the pantry, and his left leg in the washing machine. She had been especially annoyed about the pelvis under the cushions, where Lily might've seen his genitals, pink and limp. Grains of sand had collected in his belly button.

The Sertraline must've been wearing off, because Hannah had to take fourteen steps on tiptoes to get to the bathroom. She splashed water on her face, and when her facial scrub wasn't in its usual spot on the sink, she checked the bathtub. There she found John's torso, quickly stuffing a washcloth in her mouth so Lily wouldn't hear her scream. A patch of hair covered his breastbone, brown moles dotted his chest like Braille. She ran her fingers over the dots, trying to read them, searching for meaning. A person could live without ears, arms, legs, maybe even a pelvis, but you couldn't live without something as vital as your chest.

She felt for a heartbeat. Nothing. Then she pressed her ear to his sternum, the left side, the right side, silence. She pounded on his chest with her fists—*please, please, please.* Should she do CPR?

"Mom?" Lily said through the door. "I have to go pee."

Hannah pounded one last time to make it an even thirty-two, then whipped the shower curtain across the tub. "Just a minute," she said, her voice wavering. "I'll be out in a minute, sweetie." Poor Lily. She had to take her daughter to swimming lessons, follow the routine. Hannah lifted the torso with a grunt and hid it in the linen closet, covering it loosely with towels.

"Okay," Hannah said. "Come in."

Lily shuffled into the bathroom, her cheek lined from the folds of her pillow. Hannah wondered if she'd slept badly. Maybe she knew something was wrong.

"Do you want chocolate chip pancakes for breakfast?" Hannah asked through the bathroom door, deciding to make them before she got an answer. She felt compelled to make John's favorite meal as a dry run for the funeral brunch. Although pancakes would be difficult to keep warm, she thought it more important to serve what he'd enjoyed.

First Hannah checked every cupboard and the refrigerator for body parts so there weren't any surprises when Lily emerged. Then she retrieved the recipe from her file of index cards and set out the appropriate measuring cups. Finally, she gathered the flour and various ingredients she'd need. Normally she wouldn't allow such a sugary breakfast for her daughter, but the dire situation made it a necessity.

Lily sat down at the kitchen table and measured a half cup of miniature chocolate chips, as directed, while Hannah readied the pancake batter. The girl began to count each chip and ended at 101 before eating the last one.

"Chocolate, please," Hannah said. Lily scooped up the chocolate chips with care, as if they were gold nuggets, and let them fall into the batter.

"What shape would you like? Hearts? Bear paws?" Hannah asked.

Lily paused. She was a thoughtful child, sometimes too thoughtful, and that made her indecisive. Hannah prayed the girl would take after John.

"Hearts," she said, "because I love Daddy. We haven't had chocolate chip pancakes since he left."

"You're right. Let's celebrate, for Daddy. We'll pretend he's here, okay?"

"I'll set his place!" Lily said. She licked the chocolate from her fingers and went to the cupboard.

"You know, Daddy might be gone for a long time," said Hannah, testing the waters.

"How long?"

"A very long time." Hannah poured the batter onto the hot griddle, forming four lopsided hearts. The pancakes browned quickly and she flipped them.

"But not like Romeo, right?" Lily said, referring to their old cat. "He's not dead."

"I miss him too." This child was wise beyond her years. Now Hannah had lost count of how many strokes she'd mixed the remaining batter. Was it eight or nine times? She had to start over.

Hannah could smell the pancakes burning just before the smoke detector began to wail. Lily stuck her index fingers in her ears and looked to her mother for direction. The windows were already wide open. Hannah fanned the detector, and when it continued to wail, she stood on the stepladder and pulled the whole thing from the ceiling. Then she scraped the pancakes from the griddle, serving Lily the two surviving hearts. Smears of chocolate stuck to the pan. If she couldn't provide emotional nourishment, at least the girl would be well fed.

"*Bon appétit*," Hannah said. "Oh. I forgot your milk. What was I thinking?" She licked melted chocolate from her thumb. Hannah still couldn't believe John had left them. What did he expect her to do—beat her chest and tear out her hair? Throw herself on the pyre like an Indian widow? No, she would stick to routine and order. Hannah poured two tall glasses of milk.

"Mom," Lily said, looking at the pancakes, "they're burnt." She was blinking quickly, and Hannah knew she was about to cry.

"Cheerios with bananas. How does that sound?" Hannah said, despite the fact that she had more than enough batter left for a second round of pancakes. She'd have to wait for the griddle pan to cool, and even after intense scrubbing, the bitterness of burned chocolate and failure would flavor the next batch.

"Okay," Lily sniffed.

Hannah hated herself: for burning the pancakes, for making Lily cry, for letting her husband march off to war. And she hated John for thinking he could save the world, when he needed to save his own family from implosion.

Hannah dropped Lily off at the city pool sixteen minutes before her group lesson, but only after she spotted the instructor. She knew other parents did it sometimes, not that this fact made her feel less guilty—the water would be cold this early in the morning. But Hannah needed time to find the missing pieces of her husband.

As soon as she returned home, Hannah checked the linen closet. She lifted his torso and carried it to her walk-in closet to join the other body parts. In fact, she had an odd number now and she wanted to know what to do. Hannah waited for a repetitive behavior to become clear—whatever would prevent future calamity. Nothing. She still felt foggy.

"What have I done?" she said aloud, opening the door again. This was her husband's body, the body that she loved, the body that had joined hers to make another little body. Hannah stroked the leg and a few curly hairs rubbed off on her fingers. Behind his knee, the skin was soft and smooth. She ran her fingers over his toes, stopping at the big one. On top of the toe, by the knuckle, yellow skin peeled away from a thick callus. It broke her heart to think he'd been uncomfortable, that his boot hadn't fit well. Hannah found a Band-Aid in her purse and smoothed it around the toe.

More than anything, she wanted to assemble a body, something tangible to bury in the ground and get on with the grieving. She had his two legs, his torso and pelvis, his two arms, all nicely symmetrical. A whole body without a head. She was terrified to think what the injured head must look like, yet she had to make the body complete.

Hannah was sure it was hiding somewhere in the house. Starting with the bedroom, she opened all the dresser drawers, checked all the shoe boxes, searched both nightstands. Maybe his head was in a more obvious place—she hadn't thought to check the hope chest. Hannah gathered the flannel sheet covering it, exposing the glossy oak grain. How cruel, she thought, to find her husband's head in the hope chest. But when she opened the heavy oak lid, all she found was her wedding dress, boxed up neatly from the cleaners.

Suddenly Hannah knew she had to put it on. She would wear the wedding dress until she heard any news. Stripping down to her underwear, and not bothering with a bra, Hannah stepped into the frothy satin. Thankfully, she'd kept herself in good shape, and the dress still fit. But she couldn't button the last three buttons without being a contortionist. Hannah undid another to make it an even four. Because she'd gained an inch around the middle and went up a cup size after having Lily, the strapless bodice stayed in place and kept her covered. That's when she heard the knock on the door.

No one ever used the front door, besides strangers, so Hannah knew the two officers had come on a house call to regretfully inform her of John's death. As Hannah trotted through the living room, the satin swished, and she felt a great wave of relief. Finally—the certainty that had eluded her.

Hannah exhaled, pulling herself together like a drawstring, cinched tight. Now, she would need a decent funeral dress. Black wool gabardine, tropical weight. She made a mental list of things to do: make their black dresses, plan a funeral, break the news to her daughter. As long as she stuck to the plan, things would be okay.

When she opened the door, she saw only one officer. He confirmed her identity and introduced himself as Major So-and-So, a Polish or Russian name that failed to stick.

"Come in!" Hannah said. "Can I get you some coffee?" She knew John was dead, so at the very least, she'd be hospitable to the bearer of bad news.

"Mrs. Cunningham, I'm afraid your husband is missing," said Major So-and-So with an appropriately contrite look on his face. "His convoy was attacked yesterday and we're still looking for him. I can assure you that our best people are on the case."

"You haven't found a body?"

"No, ma'am. We have every reason to believe that we'll find him alive."

"Every reason? Aren't there more reasons to suspect he's dead? Or tortured first and then dead?"

"I wish I had more news, ma'am. From now on, I'll be your point of contact for the casualty affairs division and act as your media liaison."

"Media liaison," Hannah echoed. She'd never considered the potential hoopla over a missing soldier. Not only would the unbearable uncertainty continue, but there'd be a bright spotlight cast over her family.

"Anniversary?" The major nodded toward her dress.

"What?" Hannah imagined press conferences and reporters and fake sympathy.

"My wife always puts on her dress, every anniversary," the

major said. "I think it's a nice tradition. Here I thought she was the only one who did that."

"Oh," Hannah said. "Yes."

"How many years?"

The phone rang, startling Hannah, who excused herself to get it. Marissa Conway's mother, Cynthia, said she could drop Lily off on their way home. Cynthia also insisted on getting the girls sandwiches at Quiznos for all their hard work swimming. Hannah thanked her profusely. Given the news that Hannah had just received, she tried to forgive herself for forgetting her own daughter.

Hannah was looking for John's head under the dust ruffle of Lily's twin bed when the girl came in.

"Why are you wearing that dress? What happened to my room?" Lily asked. She wore John's T-shirt, the heather gray one with black lettering that said simply ARMY. The shirt fell to her knees.

Before Hannah could formulate an answer, Lily said, "Oh. You're checking for monsters."

"No, I'm not, sweetie," Hannah replied. "Don't you think Mom's wedding gown is pretty?"

"Very pretty." Lily reached out to touch the skirt.

But Hannah backed away, not yet ready to see these two parts of her world intersect: her wedding and her daughter. She didn't yet have an answer for what had happened to the girl's bedroom—the overturned toy bins and her stuffed animals scattered on the ground like roadkill. So she attempted to divert Lily's attention: "I'm just looking for something I lost. How was your lesson?"

"Good. But we have to jump off the diving board tomorrow, and I don't want to."

"I know it's scary, but after that first jump, you'll be fine.

It seems like a long way down, but it's not. It's only half the height of your dad."

Still concerned about jumping from the diving board, Lily looked skeptical. Her hair hung in ropey tangles that Hannah should've been combing out.

"Mom," Lily asked, "did you forget to pick me up?"

"Of course not." Hannah couldn't show vulnerability, not at this point. She would put on a front: her Mommy-is-calm-and-nothing's-wrong face.

"Can I have a Popsicle?" Lily asked. Either the girl was no longer worried, or remained worried but wanted to take advantage of Hannah's new, relaxed attitude toward sugar.

"Sure. I'm going to put everything back and clean, so why don't you watch *The Last Unicorn?*"

Hannah waited until she heard the familiar opening scene of the DVD, then returned to the walk-in closet, still without John's head.

"John?" she said to the collection of flesh. "John, can you hear me? I can't do this anymore."

Hannah realized that she had to put him back together before she could have a funeral. She'd simply sew him up with sturdy thread, then she'd have a body, and she could get on with the grieving. So she gathered several large needles and dental floss, which she thought would be sturdy enough. Starting with the right leg, she lined the skin up with the skin of his hip and sewed a running whipstitch. Expecting nothing short of perfection, she made even, precise stitches. She was pleased that the white dental floss looked less monstrous than dark thread. It would do nicely.

Hannah hummed as she worked, usually "Over the Rainbow," careful to create strong bonds, joining skin to skin. She

wanted to rush to completion, get it over with, but careless-
ness wouldn't bring John back.

Working into the evening, she pacified Lily with a DVD of
Bambi and butterscotch pudding and a pillow fort she allowed
the girl to sleep in. After all, Hannah couldn't send Lily back
to her ransacked bedroom. Back in the privacy of the walk-in
closet, the exact, neat stitches brought Hannah comfort, and
she kept count through the night, getting past four hundred.
She was pleased that her handiwork held fast.

After sewing everything together, she checked the seams
again, which held tight. All she had left were a few stitches
around his shoulder, and in the end, Hannah counted 482
stitches. The absent head annoyed her. In any case, she could
live without finding it—she had a body now. John was dead.

Hannah heard rustling coming from the living room. She
vaguely remembered seeing the light filter through the windows but the adrenaline had kept her sewing. The clock on the
nightstand read 7:34 A.M. and Lily would be getting up soon.
Hannah rolled the body back into the closet as quickly as she
could—she had to get back to the morning routine. Breakfast
and swimming lessons.

It wasn't easy leveraging his weight into the oak chest, but
it eventually went in. Hannah grabbed a leg, bent it at the knee
to make it fit, and tucked it inside. She did the same for the
other leg, his pelvis, torso, everything. There, she thought,
done.

Lily babbled in the car, as she often did when she was nervous.
Hannah had already stopped the incessant questions about the
wedding dress by threatening a spanking, which she'd never
actually done.

"How high is it really?" Lily asked.

"Half of your dad, remember?" Hannah said. She slipped off her sandals and drove barefoot. The skirt of her dress was so big that sitting on it made her a full two inches taller in the driver's seat. She liked this vantage point.

"I mean how many feet high?" asked Lily.

"Maybe four? I don't know, honey." If Hannah had to guess, she liked four feet, or forty-eight inches.

"Exactly four feet, or more than that?"

"You'll be fine." She glanced at Lily in the rearview mirror. The girl was pulling on her swimsuit strap, letting it snap on her neck. Hannah had to focus on Lily now and her daughter must learn how to swim. What if there came a time when Lily fell from a boat or the car crashed into an icy river or her plane landed in the ocean? She had to know how to swim for unexpected emergencies. It was a potentially lifesaving skill: making order from chaos.

Hannah was surprised to find no one else at the pool, until she realized they were forty minutes early. The main entrance was locked, but the women's locker room wasn't. She took Lily's hand and they walked by the toilets and showers, despite Lily asking twice if they were supposed to do this. The turquoise water sparkled from the morning sun and chlorine.

"Shh," Hannah said. "I think you should practice the jump first so you're not nervous when the time comes."

"Are you sure?" Lily asked.

"Yes. And I'll be right here if you need me. I know you can do it, sweetie."

The girl began to climb the ladder until she reached the top. As she walked to the edge of the blue diving board, Hannah could hear the girl counting each step, stopping at seven. Lily tiptoed back to the ladder and started over, taking smaller steps to the edge and ending at eight.

What compulsions was she teaching their daughter? Were

the compulsions genetic, or was the girl learning from her environment? Hannah realized that if John was everything good, and Hannah was always the opposite parent, then she was bad. The devil in the details. Maybe she was the monster, the one who'd lost her head. How could she abandon all hope?

"Wait just a sec, honey." Hannah reached into her purse, found the bottle of Sertraline, and swallowed one without water. "Okay, you can go. Remember you're my brave girl and you can do it!"

Hannah too would have to muster courage. To have hope. Like fear, hope was a messy emotion. What *could* happen. John *could* have been taken in by an Iraqi family, who were too scared to reveal they'd harbored an American soldier. John *could* have a severe concussion and temporary amnesia, lying confused in a British field hospital. Or John *could* be hiding in the desert scrub, using his knowledge of botany to survive.

Hannah imagined all the yellow ribbons that would appear around town, tied to trees and pinned to T-shirts. Patriotic signs that declared PRAY FOR JOHN and USA LOVES JOHN. The photo of him in desert fatigues that the local Walmart would print for free, thousands of copies to be plastered everywhere, including the pool's bulletin board. The casseroles people would drop off at the house, so many that Hannah wouldn't have to cook for months. And the cake, decorated as an American flag, with blueberries and strawberries and white frosting.

Lily stepped off the edge, not really jumping but allowing her body to fall. A splash. The girl surfaced, triumphant, and began to tread water.

"You should swim too, Mom!" Lily shouted.

Hannah kicked off her sandals, and with the dress billowing around her, jumped in.

Salt of the Earth

SPECIAL THANKS TO the Abbott Creek Public Library for letting us make copies of this unofficial bulletin. We know that versions of the story are still circulating at the Bluebird, Skeeter's Tavern, Shear Beauty, and All Saints Lutheran. Even two years out, it's important that everyone has the same information. We want to squash any lingering jealousy and reiterate that all the crazy behaviors were a direct result of the love virus. Again, *no one* is to blame here.

Apparently there's a young journalist sniffing around town again, what with the two-year anniversary. We should be proud of our tight-lipped reserve but we can't rest on our laurels. We take care of our own and damned if we're going to let Twittering or the YouTube air our dirty laundry. What happens in Abbott Creek stays in Abbott Creek. Needless to say, once you've read this, please destroy it.

So, where to start? Probably with patient zero, identity still unknown to the scientists. We think it was Tami Holtz. Sure, she was as innocuous as the Jell-O salads she brought to church potlucks—though, truth be told, few in the congregation have a taste for canned fruit and hazmat-orange gelatin anymore.

Some of you remember almost a decade back, when her husband Al was crushed under the tires of his International. (A fine man, loyal to Case International, because the dealership a mile south of town employs five of our own. Screw John Deere.) So when Tami, a teller at the bank, cashed the first Social Security check for Wilbur Donaldson and he took her out to lunch at the Bluebird Café (arguably the finest dining establishment of the three options), we all thought, good for her. Al Holtz was a fine man but ten years of mourning was more than fair.

Those of us who've been around long enough remember that she was heartbroken long before Al's accident. They couldn't have children and Tami had decided on a little girl from some country we could barely pronounce—Belize? Nicaragua?—cute as a button but we did wonder to ourselves about how Tami would tame that curly hair. Somehow or another, the birth mother changed her mind, and Tami and Al returned with nothing but stories about monkeys blocking the road and trying to peel spiky fruit they were served for breakfast. It just wasn't meant to be after all, they said, shrugging and smiling. But their eyes betrayed them. Al wasn't much of a drinker, but one year, on the night before Thanksgiving, he'd had one too many beers at Skeeter's Tavern and he told her name to anyone who'd listen: "Amelia. My baby girl. And we were going to call her Mimi."

All in all, with no kids and a long-dead husband, Tami could've used some joy in her life. When she found it in Wilbur Donaldson, we were all happy too. They started playing bridge and pinochle with two other couples—the Smiths (Terry and Peg) and the McLaughlins (Paul and Jane). One evening Tami hosted, serving sloppy joes, pigs in a blanket,

and Wilbur's favorite drink, Seven and Sevens. The next morning both Terry and Paul failed to show up at the Bluebird coffee hour to talk about the decreased price per bushel on corn
and two full weeks with only three-tenths of an inch of rain.

Turned out that the Smiths and the McLaughlins got sick,
some stomach thing. Peg suspected the pigs in a blanket, those
innocent little wieners wrapped in flaky, buttery Pillsbury
dough. It's always the most delicious little bits that turn out to
be sinful.

Speaking of sinful, we eventually deduced that Tami had
kissed Terry and/or Paul, Wilbur had kissed Jane and/or Peg,
or maybe the ladies were kissing each other. As long as no kids
were involved and it happened behind closed doors, it's really none of our business. For example, we're well aware that
Jeanine Yoder and Beth Peterson are more than "roommates,"
but that's their concern. Our state was one of the first to legal-
ize ladies together and men together, if that's what they want.
Before New York, even. When interviewed, we'd just shrug
and say, "To each his own."

Anyway, the Smiths and the McLaughlins started acting as
moony as Tami and Wilbur. Lovesick puppies all around. They
went to the county courthouse in Miles so Tami and Wilbur
could make it official, and they came back to the Bluebird,
Wilbur paying for all the customers' dinners because his new
bride was "the most beautiful to ever walk this earth." Then
Paul and Jane renewed their vows, right there in front of the
salad bar with iceberg lettuce and bacon bits, not to mention
the soup of the day, Wisconsin cheddar. Terry didn't bother
with any formalities and had his tongue down Peg's throat in
no time, almost tipping her out of her chair. And Peg was no
small lady. Always had been a husky girl, even when she was
showing the family's prize steers at the State Fair.

We can't figure out exactly what happened next, except

that Dick Maas (yeah, the kids learning Spanish in school had a good time with that name), that old Dick Maas, tighter than the steering on a new Silverado, left a twenty on the table. He told the waitress, seventeen-year-old Madison Bessel (J.T.'s daughter), to "keep the change, gorgeous." We wish we could say that girl knew something wasn't right, but she got infected too. She swatted his hand—the one holding the twenty, not the one holding his cane—and said, "Dick Maas, you know I can't take your money." To which he replied, "You're worth every penny," and she said, "Now, Dick Maas, are you flirting with me?" and he answered, "Only if the pretty lady likes it."

We have it on good authority that this exchange took place, but we're not sure how either of them caught the lovesickness. Who was in (ahem) intimate contact with the McLaughlins or the Smiths? Of course, when the scientists first came to town, trying to find the first person who had the virus and how it spread and all that, they wanted to know every detail and investigated all the food at the Bluebird first. Took samples of everything in the salad bar, from the cottage cheese to the bacon bits, swabbed the Plexiglas and everything. They took the hamburger buns and frozen cod fillets and even the coffee grounds.

But we digress. Dick Maas's neighbor, Sandy Rademacher, who checked in on him every other day, said she had to open a childproof prescription bottle for him, one filled with little blue pills, and if she wasn't mistaken, weren't those pills for naughty times? She always was a good Catholic and had a penchant for self-punishment. We suspect that she caught the bug too, but she refused to leave her house. The only people she let visit were Father Galligan and Thelma Rothschild, who we all know is the town's gossip if there ever was one. She cut hair in her beauty parlor, retrofitted from a sun porch, but denies she ever caught the virus herself. Hard to tell, since she was always a little moony to begin with, and we're not sure she was ever entirely faithful to her husband, Bill.

Right, Dick Maas and his little conquest, Madison Bessel. Her Grand Am had been parked in his driveway overnight (twice) before her father, J.T., decided that denial wasn't the best coping mechanism. The story goes that he made sure Madison was working the breakfast shift at the Bluebird and he went over to Dick Maas's house with his twelve-gauge in the footwell of the passenger seat of his F-150, a gun he normally used to shoot raccoons in the barn or corncrib. The rest of the encounter we have to imagine, since there were no eyewitnesses.

"Morning, Dick."

"Hi there, J.T. You already on your second cutting of alfalfa?" (Dick had been outside, ambling to his mailbox.)

"Sure am. Listen, Dick, I need some information. You know my youngest girl means the world to me, right?"

"Of course. That Madison's outstanding. Good work ethic."

(Here we're certain that J.T. winced. She was headed to Iowa State in the fall, unlike many of her peers, who'd be attending the nearest community college.)

"Well, I'd do anything for her," J.T. replied. "You understand that I have to protect her."

"As any father would."

"I won't act without proof. I'll be straight here, Dick, and only ask once. Have you been intimate with my seventeen-year-old daughter?"

Whatever Dick's answer was, either J.T. didn't like it, or he didn't believe it. He retrieved the shotgun from the F-150 and *boom!*

No, no, don't jump to conclusions. We're not the murdering type. J.T. shot a slug just above the brass address numbers affixed to the front of the house, 109 for 109 West Street. The slug went through the siding and, we imagine, Dick's living room. Just enough to scare him and make the neighbors wonder. At least that's how we think it went down. The slug is still there, the vinyl siding cracked where it entered.

Something tells us that it didn't happen as expected because not only did Madison and Dick keep sharing the same bed, but J.T. got infected too. This much we do know: he climbed the ladder to the top of the water tower and proclaimed that if Deanne (Koenig, the Lutheran pastor's wife) didn't love him, he'd jump. It was all documented in the firemen's report.

The volunteer fire crew, waiting patiently at the bottom, sent up Captain Matt Schoenfelt to try and talk him down. They tried everything short of sending Deanne Koenig up to meet her high school sweetheart. Anyway, Matt Schoenfelt climbed up, a little winded by the time he reached the top, and asked J.T. point-blank what it would take to get him down.

According to the log report, J.T. said, "Love. Love is all you need." We think Matt gave him a bear hug, maybe even a kiss, but it was hard to tell that far up, and honestly, we needed our glasses to see anything accurately, at least from our vantage point on the ground. In the end, J.T. came down on the ladder, even without Deanne Koenig there to persuade him.

Afterward, the volunteer firemen had a beer at Skeeter's, just two Budweisers each because they were still on call. Even before J.T. was drunk from all the rounds they bought him, he was hugging everyone in sight. Real hugs, not the quick kind where you just touch shoulders and tap the back, both people nervous to get it over with, but big, genuine embraces where even your navels touch, your halves squishing together, arms wrapped around the other person's back and squeezing until it's hard to breathe.

The scientists later told us that oxytocin, the feel-good,

bonding hormone, is released when you hug someone. But the main rush of oxytocin occurs at the peak of, you know, when you're intimate. That did a lot to explain some of the more unusual pairings, like Madison Bessel and Dick Maas, not to mention what we suspect of J.T. Bessel and his savior, fire chief Matt Schoenfelt.

At Skeeter's, all the firemen, when they weren't hugging and smiling, had an informal discussion about the main item on the agenda for their next meeting. Jillian Meyer, longtime assistant for Doc Levin, needed a new heart. She had some kind of congenital problem that up until then could be managed with medication. Every month, she had to drive the two hours to the university hospital to see a specialist. Even if they could find a suitable donor, that kind of surgery was ungodly expensive.

You better believe the firefighters were discussing the upcoming benefit. Since they always hosted the annual Pancake Supper at the Legion Hall to raise money for the town's emergency services, they had all the supplies and know-how to prepare the food for Jillian's fund-raiser. They knew exactly how to mix the batter, how much of it was necessary to pour on the griddle for each pancake, and how to cook the sausages just right. Not to mention how much butter, syrup, orange juice, milk, and coffee they'd need. They also knew which businesses to approach for donations to the silent auction (Buch Hardware and Teasdale Chevrolet would be big donors, but the Abbott Creek Quick Stop, not so much). In the end, we all helped out in some way, even if it was only paying the $8 for our plate of pancakes.

Jillian got a new heart, her family didn't go bankrupt, and Doc Levin kept his only employee. Most of us have a story or two about how Jillian had calmed our temperamental tabby or helped a young cow during a difficult delivery. At the time, everyone agreed to avoid contact with Jillian, in case this sickness really was contagious and could weaken her poor ticker.

Speaking of hearts, the next one affected by the virus was Skeeter's wife, the bartender herself. She'd always been generous with her pours, especially the whiskey. She had the stomach thing the next day, and when she returned to her post behind the bar, everybody got doubles on the house. Even Luke Baker, who already had two drunk-driving charges—a third would revoke his license and he wouldn't be able to operate his farm machinery—got poured a double of his usual, Royal Velvet, on the rocks. A fourth-generation Abbott Creek farmer, just twenty years old then, his red face partially obscured by the rounded bill of his green Pioneer Seed cap.

Skeeter's wife, Kasey, kept pouring the doubles for him, bending over the bar every chance she got to show off her cleavage, which wasn't half bad for a middle-aged woman who'd lived fast and hard. Thankfully, Skeeter was visiting his mother up in Minnesota, so he wasn't around to see his wife's flirtation. Rumor has it that Kasey and Luke Baker snuck off to the bathroom together, but if there's any storyteller not to be trusted, it's a regular of Skeeter's Tavern. Sure, Luke seemed too young for Kasey, if you ask us, but nobody asked.

The next spectacle happened at the Little League game against Conway. Mulhausen's son, Timothy, the mentally challenged one or whatever people are calling it these days—well, Timothy was up to bat. (He was fifteen but they stuck him in Little League rather than Pony League because of his ability, or lack thereof.) The Conway pitcher (and team) knew full well what he was supposed to do, and he threw the softest, slowest, most gentle pitch, but it hardly made it over the plate. Umpire called a ball.

Everyone knew where this was headed. The pitcher was supposed to throw three more balls so Timothy would get walked and get on first base and feel like he'd accomplished something. But on the second pitch, Timothy actually hit the ball, a pop fly to center field. The poor center fielder didn't know if he was supposed to catch it, and in the time it took him to make a decision, he let the ball drop in front of him. The right fielder took his time, because people were still yelling at Timothy to run to first base. He'd never had a hit before and therefore didn't know to run. By the time he touched the bag (with his feet and hands, no less), Lisa Sanders was standing up on the bleachers, screaming her lungs out in celebration.

Yes, that Lisa Sanders, the rising sophomore already on the varsity cheerleading squad at Dexter. Some of you may remember when the districts consolidated thirty years ago and the kids were bussed to Dexter. In a twist of redistricting irony, the Dexter Demons spiritually annihilated the old Abbott Creek Crusaders. Anyway, *that* Lisa Sanders, with wavy locks the color of a newborn fawn and the body of a calendar girl, who'd visited untold numbers of Abbott Creek boys in their fantasies and more than a few Abbott Creek men as well.

"Way to go, Timmy!" she yelled in her megaphone cheerleader voice. Then: *"That's my boy!"* And before we knew it, she was out on the field, and when she got to first base — Timothy grinning as usual, and squawking to boot — Lisa Sanders kissed him square on the lips. Timothy, knowing he'd scored a symbolic home run, followed her back to the dugout. The rest of the team (remember these were fifth grade boys who barely knew how to zip their flies) started giving her crap. "It's my turn, Lisa" and "Hey, Lisa, what about me?" and "I got a triple, Lisa, so what's that worth to ya?"

Lisa Sanders, for her part, put a hand on each hip, right at the belt loops of her exquisite denim cutoffs, and shouted: "I don't care what you think. I'm in love. There, I said it. I love Timothy Mulhausen!"

Of course, this elicited further squawking from Timothy. For the rest of us, though, it was a turning point and we started our investigation in earnest. Lisa was clearly stricken by a serious malady. The others we could brush off as summer flings, to be forgotten by the time the leaves change color. But Lisa Sanders making out with the retarded kid? Don't get us wrong, Timothy's a sweet, kind soul we all look out for, but Lisa usually went for three-sport athletes like Blake Nelson or Devin Schrader.

Poor Blake. We'll always remember Private First Class Nelson and his courageous service in Iraq. He was always a hellraiser, starting with his long-suffering mother and ending with Mrs. Taubs, the math instructor who refused to let him pass Algebra II (but she was new to teaching). He may've been a problem child, but when he put that excess energy into sports or defending our country, we couldn't be more proud of the boy. His portrait, looking handsome and serious in his dress uniform, hangs just inside the entrance of the Legion Hall.

But we digress. Right, Lisa Sanders and Timothy Mulhausen. No one could find the connection—how did Lisa catch it? We started thinking maybe it was the water or the food, because it's not like either of them hung out at Skeeter's Tavern or with the bridge and pinochle crowd. Madison Bessel, maybe? Just imagining Madison and Lisa Sanders together got some of us hot and bothered, before we reminded ourselves they could be our daughters. For shame.

The city manager—not that a town of less than a thousand people constituted a city—but the city manager, Joel Schwartzendruber, decided to conduct some extra tests on the water supply. When he didn't find anything out of the ordinary, he made sure to tell the coffee-hour crowd at the Bluebird. A little more nitrogen than usual, from the spring fertilizer and pesticide runoff, but that was to be expected this time of year.

Word got out from Eddie Callahan, who ran the Abbott Creek Meat Locker, that the steers kept trying to nuzzle him, or sometimes try to hump him, at the moment of their demise—that is, when he approached with the stun gun. Some of the conspiracy theorists (of which there are maybe three) think Tami Holtz, when she served that ground beef in the sloppy joes at that infamous couples bridge night, gave out contaminated meat. In turn, from a lovesick steer that had been slaughtered by Eddie Callahan. We admit that's not entirely far-fetched, but it makes our stomachs turn just thinking about it.

By this time, summer waned and Labor Day weekend approached, which means Heritage Days (renamed from Sauerkraut Days after World War II, as some of you know). Always a good time, when everybody comes together for the parade and carnival and tractor pull. Not to mention the free sauerkraut and wieners, handed out right after the parade, on Saturday at 11 A.M. in the park pavilion. And every year one of the boosters, usually Chuck Appleby, draws a grid of numbers in sidewalk chalk on the street, makes a little pen with steel gates, and sticks a steer inside to drop manure on the lucky number.

There were a couple of rumblings, warnings that maybe we should've canceled or at least scaled down the festivities, because a handful more people had caught the lovesickness. What if it spread with so many people in close contact, sharing cotton candy, licking their sticky fingers, maybe even puking after too many rides on the Sizzler? That happened once in a while, especially if the parents were in the beer tent and let their sons loose with friends. There was probably more danger of contagion in the beer tent, anyway. Of course we'd never cancel Heritage Days—the kids looked forward to it all year. No one had actually gotten hurt from the virus, unless you counted the assault on our senses when we saw the various odd couples. People were just more open about their displays of affection.

The show must go on, and it did. We were careful to choose former postmaster Earl Halsted as grand marshal of the parade, since he showed no symptoms—stoic as ever, never got too excited. Even during the holiday rush at the post office, he handled every package with care while the rest of us tried to spit that nasty envelope glue from our tongues. All the grand marshal had to do was wave and throw Tootsie Rolls from the back of the convertible, a courtesy loan from Teasdale Chevrolet. Earl was in fine form that morning, serving as de facto town ambassador. Members of the American Legion marching as the color guard, our volunteer EMTs waving from the ambulance and the fire truck with sirens blaring, the Dexter Demons marching band playing mostly on tempo, the classic cars so shiny you could see your reflection in the hood. In other words, the whole nine yards.

It wasn't until Earl's convertible approached the judges' stand, at the end of Locust Street, that it happened. Instead of continuing that dignified wave, he stood up in the backseat and started dancing. Thrusting his arthritic hips and wiggling in his khaki trousers, singing the James Brown song "I Feel Good."

"*Nana nana nana na*, SO GOOD," *bum, bum*—he indicated those two beats by sticking his butt out to the rhythm—"SO GOOD"—two more butt shakes—"I GOT YOU!"

The object of his affection appeared to be Gladys Fogleberg, an honorary judge this year, honorary because we didn't know if she could actually see the floats (her son Don picked her up from the nursing home in Miles that morning so she could be around for what most assumed would be her last Heritage Days, which she still called Sauerkraut Days). Admittedly, we were relieved Earl hadn't chosen one of the Sauer-kraut Queen candidates in the cars behind him. They were just high school girls, trying to come up with answers to your basic pageant-style questions: What issue will be most impor-tant for our state in this millennium? If you could go back in time and meet one person, who would it be and why?

The previous year Madison Bessel had won, advocating for more ethanol production and wanting to meet Eleanor Roos-evelt. Since Dick Maas's house was on the parade route, they sat outside in lawn chairs, holding hands and watching the floats roll by. Afterward, she put on a cobalt-blue sundress and her sash and tiara to go crown the next queen.

Oh, that dancing Earl Halsted and his paramour, Gladys Fo-gleberg—she wasn't about to turn down any attention. Since he was grand marshal, he'd be the first in line for the wieners and sauerkraut. But he wheeled Gladys up to the pavilion, so technically she was first in line. If we didn't know any better, we might think the way she ate those hot dogs to be lewd. But she was a ninety-two-year-old woman with dentures so that kind of thing couldn't be helped. She was smitten with Earl too, her crackling, joyful laugh rising above the general din.

Obviously we were worried that everyone who ate the wie-ners and sauerkraut would catch the lovesickness, but that didn't appear to be the case. Still seemed to be transmitted by individuals. The children, thank God, were completely unaf-fected. Only those who'd reached puberty were susceptible. Lisa Sanders, who was vying for the crown this year, said on-stage that she's already met the most intriguing person in his-tory, the boy of her dreams, and he lived right here in Abbott Creek. We all silently groaned when we realized she meant Timothy, the special boy.

Since it was impossible to predict who would be next, we stopped trying. All we knew was that Pastor Koenig's wife,

Deanne, and Skeeter (of the infamous tavern, back from Minnesota) were playing tonsil hockey while she was supposed to be running the ring toss booth. Scandalous, yes, but no more so than the other crazy couples. We were less surprised and more interested in seeing who Pastor Koenig would hook up with. Turned out to be Misty Lovell, who kept the books for Buch Hardware, lived in a trailer just east of town, and had three kids by two different fathers. Love, as they say, is blind.

By that evening, when the street dance started in front of the fire station, it was one big orgy of people hugging and rubbing and kissing. The kids had been put to bed, crashing from their sugar highs and already dreaming about next year's Heritage Days. On that concrete pad outside the fire station, none of the social conventions mattered one bit, so long as no one got jealous. Even if they did, the jealousy didn't last long before they started showing symptoms themselves. Joy hummed in the air and love intoxicated our bodies, flushed with warmth.

We should've known the golden hour wouldn't last long. The next morning, when we woke up beside the person we'd recently discovered was the love of our life, we turned on the TV to see the weather report. If there was rain forecasted, the tractor pull would be more exciting, with mud and all. The local news, out of Cedar Rapids, was on, and the Ken doll anchor said, "Stay tuned for our special report on a virus sweeping the hamlet of Abbott Creek."

We did stay tuned, and what we saw killed the mood faster than morning breath. Some nosy reporter, probably called by an out-of-towner visiting for Heritage Days, was reporting live from our park pavilion. Standing amid the discarded tickets, glow sticks, and foil potato chip bags (the Lutheran youth group hadn't collected the trash yet), the reporter said, "An unknown sexually transmitted virus has affected nearly sixty percent of the town's residents. Symptoms include irrational behavior, heart palpitations, and mania."

We tried to ignore the biased "reporting" but our racing thoughts made it difficult to enjoy the tractor pull. Who were they to unfairly judge us? That wet-eared reporter was using us for a chance at the big time. At the tractor pull, we decided no one would talk. We'd stay indoors to halt the spread of the sickness, but under no circumstances would anyone give out information. We refused to feed the vultures. Sure enough, the next day, the national media swooped in.

In the meantime, that evening after the tractor pull, tragedy was narrowly averted by a couple who disobeyed the stay-home quarantine. The volunteers on call that night—Denny Weiser, Melanie Strickland, and Clarence Cecak—arrived at the scene in the ambulance, expecting the worst. The front end of the Ford Taurus (we don't buy foreign) was embracing that giant oak just west of Mulhausen's dairy. Melanie Strickland crossed herself and Clarence Cecak said a quick prayer, because they were longtime veterans of the ambulance service and in their years had seen a number of bad wrecks. They had, in Melanie's words, "picked up pieces of people you know." Awful that not only was there nothing they could do in some cases except collect body parts, but they also knew exactly who the parts belonged to. For example, they knew it was Pastor Koenig's girl's head of permed blond hair (a tractor trailer slowed in dense fog and the Koenig girl drove right under it) just like they recognized it was Al Holtz's torso (crushed under the combine tire) and legs (clad in Carhartt dungarees, ten feet back in the field).

Well, it turned out the Taurus was a newer model that had both front- and side-impact air bags, and the couple in question, Amy Buch and Roger "Smitty" Smith, were scratched up and Amy got a friction burn on her cheek from the air bag, but by some miracle (after Denny Weiser used the Jaws of Life to cut them out) they were both fine. It was only then that the EMTs noticed that Smitty's Levis were around his knees, buck naked from the waist down. His manhood, thankfully for him, was left unscathed. And then Melanie Strickland noticed the burn on Amy's face (who'd been in the passenger seat) was on her right cheek, as if she'd been twisted toward the driver. We'll let your imagination figure out exactly what those two were doing when they hit the tree.

Of course, news of the accident spread quickly and it became a cautionary tale for the entire town. We stayed inside and let the virus run its course. Kept our mouths shut. It was probably for the best, to be honest. Harvest time would be here before we knew it and we had to be at the top of our game to get the highest yields. No point in mooning around when there's work to be done.

Didn't stop the news media, though. Much worse than even caucus time, when the presidential candidates pander to us and the rest of the country wonders why our rural flyover state gets to pick the leader of the free world. Some journalist deemed us "good people, salt-of-the-earth types" and it stuck. Named our sickness the SOTE virus, for salt of the earth. Which was much better than calling it "the love disease" or "the horny illness." A few whack jobs even proposed that it could actually be a cure for all the hate in the world, a tool that could bring peace to conflict areas. Bring different groups of people together, like the Israelis and the Palestinians.

Don't look at us — we didn't say it. But reverse biological weapons, spreading love instead of hate, sounds pretty good if you think about it. Impossible, but not a bad notion. If we thought it would actually work, we would've given the scientists more information.

Of course, they appeared about the same time as the journalists. The scientists didn't believe us when we said, "What strange behavior? No, nothing out of the ordinary." We dutifully rolled up our sleeves and let them poke needles in our veins and collect our blood. After all, we were reasonable people. In some of the samples, they found unknown antibodies and increased levels of oxytocin, the love and bonding hormone.

They also found, from Madison Bessel's blood, that she was pregnant. We weren't thrilled to hear that news, but she'd already deferred her enrollment to spend more time with Dick Maas. By the time she started showing, the media were long gone. The scientists had left their contact info with us, just in case there were any "new developments," which, of course, there weren't.

Madison Bessel ended up commuting to a junior college near Cedar Rapids while raising the baby girl with Dick. Got an associate's degree in accounting in just two semesters and took over the finances at the Case International dealership. That little girl was the spitting image of her mother, always happy and smiling, climbing on the farm equipment when Madison wasn't looking.

So there you have it. That's pretty much where the story ends. No need for jealousy or the blame game. Things turned out alright, so take this newsletter and destroy it before some journalist gets his paws on it.

One last thing: remember how the company transferred Madison and her family to a bigger dealership in Missouri? But also remember how they came back, not six months later. Turns out, this isn't a bad place to live. And that's another little secret we plan to keep.

Modern Medicine

R ITA CERTAINLY WASN'T the only nurse to self-med-
icate — some of her coworkers in the burn unit chose
wine or Xanax. Who would deny her the occasional line of
blow, especially after what she saw every day? These days she
preferred ketamine, so when she was down in San Diego for
a conference, she enlisted one of the younger girls to go to
Tijuana with her.

Rita was already regretting her decision. On the trolley to
the border crossing, Ashley gyrated against the steel pole.

"Think I made the wrong career choice?" Ashley said.

"You'd need fake nails." Rita eyed the girl's fingernails,
neatly trimmed like all their coworkers', to avoid harboring
bacteria. On 8 West, their patients' immune systems were as
fragile and precarious as eggshells. The slightest disturbance
might cause an irreparable crack.

"My passport photo is hideous. Do you want to see it? It's
so awful," Ashley said.

"I believe you."

"Honestly, Rita, you're hilarious. Is it true that you got into med school?"

Rita was used to seeing Ashley in standard blue scrubs, and she looked like a teenager in the denim skirt and flip-flops. How did anyone take this girl seriously?

"Sure," Rita said. "I did. But you can't kill anyone if you're a nurse."

"You killed a patient? Really?"

"You're not listening—it was the fear of killing someone. You make a bad diagnosis and someone dies," Rita said. "I don't want that kind of responsibility." She pinched the bridge of her nose to stave off a headache. It was a partial lie. Nurses could kill people by forgetting to scrub their hands between patients or failing to change gloves or even by wearing street clothes in the clinical setting. Bacteria posed a constant threat in the burn unit, an invisible enemy that invaded the body through vulnerable, skinless flesh.

"I understand," Ashley said. "That would haunt me forever."

Rita had her own ghosts, and they weren't the patients who sent her tiger lilies and daisies after their hospital stay. There was nothing modern medicine could do for patients like Cal Bishop. They could only make him comfortable with plenty of morphine, the standard of care for decades, and hope the antibiotic cocktail would kill the mutating bacteria. He'd gotten the infection from the hospital. Instead of healing, the hospital made him sicker.

Rita and Ashley joined the line for the pedestrian border crossing, a bridge that snaked across the dusty landscape, above the mess of cars trying to get through, everything the dull color of dry earth.

"That's why we try to forget," Ashley was saying, "with some help from our friend Special K."

Rita felt a pang of tenderness for the girl and regretted that she'd misjudged Ashley. "Better living through chemistry, right?" Rita said.

"That is so true."

"You're a little young to be jaded."

"I'm just mature for my age. Being on 8 West makes you grow up fast," Ashley said, referring to the burn unit. "I know way too many dead people."

"You'll get used to that," said Rita, trying to hide the cynicism in her voice.

As they approached the border guards and immigration, Rita went first, flashed her passport, answered the requisite questions. She'd been to Canada and the Caribbean but never Mexico. She folded her arms and waited for Ashley. On this side of the bridge, just steps from the border, children begged for coins. An infant girl, barely old enough to stay upright, sat on a yellow blanket, propped against the safety wall with a tiny guitar strapped to her chest. No parents in sight, just a used paper cup for money. Ashley let out a whimper.

Can't save them all, Rita thought. They saw their fair share of abuse cases, like the kid with the so-called red kneesocks — scald burns up his legs. Who would dip a child in boiling water? The question still arose for Rita, but these days she didn't attempt to answer it.

A chestnut-colored mutt trailed one of the beggar kids. When the boy approached Rita, the dog sat at attention, watching the boy the entire time.

"*Tu perro?*" she asked, dusting off her college Spanish.

"*Sí,*" said the boy, and then continued but Rita didn't understand.

"*Por el perro,*" she said, tucking a five-dollar bill into his palm. She felt guilty for missing Beau's birthday — she meant to go to the doggy bakery and buy a cake for him before she left but never got around to it. Suddenly, the children swarmed her.

Cal Bishop had fallen for her quicker than most patients. He'd been on the unit for two days before declaring his love, and he was in high spirits despite the fact that she'd come to do burn care, a euphemism for excruciating procedures like peeling back the dressings and scraping away dead tissue. She'd seen grown men beg for mercy. The comatose patients were the lucky ones on this unit.

"Rita, what if you're the great love of my life?" He was nineteen and insisted on wearing a pristine White Sox hat. He left the brim flat and square, which made it look like an old man's cap.

"Well then," she replied, hanging a new bag of saline, "like all great loves, it will be unrequited."

"You're cruel. But I still love you."

"You only love me because I give you opioids. The synapses in your brain are confused." Under her sterile gown and scrub top, sweat pricked her armpits. The patient rooms were kept hot to help maintain normal body temperatures. The staff of 8 West was constantly debating which brands of deodorant worked best, like Mitchum or Arrid. It didn't matter, really, since their patients' wounds often had a decaying, putrid odor.

"Rita, I know almost everything about you. You love blueberry yogurt and your black Lab, whose name is Beau. You tuck that Celexa pen behind your ear and twirl it when you're bored. And you wear a 34C bra size, right?"

"Cal." She had no idea how he knew such an intimate detail. He'd never seen her without several layers of clothing. Yet she was secretly flattered that he'd taken the care to find out.

"I'm right, aren't I?"

"If I tell you, will this be the end of this particular discussion?"

"I swear." He winced as Rita peeled soaked gauze from his bloated hands. His fingers resembled charred ballpark hot dogs. The burns on his hands were more severe than those of his chest and torso, because he'd used them to put out the flames.

"How did you know?" Rita asked.

"I got Danielle to check the stuff in your locker. She loves me."

"So that's what you know about me? Don't you want to know the bad stuff?"

"Nope. You'll always be a saint. Itch my nose?" he said. Rita used a gloved hand to do so. "And we have plenty of time to get to know each other."

"Okay, stud." Rita loved the way he looked at her, a forty-year-old woman, with a mixture of admiration and lust.

"Cool," he said. "Is stud my pet name?"

Rita and Ashley bought the ketamine from a shady *farmacia* at a ridiculous markup. But since it was what they came for, and she'd been working extra shifts lately, Rita didn't mind. Ashley just shrugged.

"What's next?" the girl said.

"Tequila," Rita replied.

They settled on a patio bar with festive umbrellas and yellow sunflowers stuffed in recycled green wine bottles. Rita ordered a margarita on the rocks, no salt, while Ashley got a piña colada.

"So," Ashley said. "Do you just put it in your drink?"

Rita shaded her eyes from the afternoon sun. "You've never done K before?" The girl was full of contradictions.

"I usually just pop a Xanax or Ativan."

"Put it under your tongue," Rita said, tilting her head back to demonstrate. "It's bitter, but just let it absorb. Don't try to swallow."

"Sublingual," Ashley said. "I never thought of that."

"Well," Rita said, standing. She refused to wait for her drink. At the same time, she didn't know how to end her interaction with Ashley. "Well, I'm off to meet God."

Rita made her way to the bathroom. The walls were bright orange like construction signs, the kind that warn people to slow down. She took the vial from her purse and poured half the liquid under her tongue. Rita closed her eyes, letting the wave crash into her. When it hit, she felt buoyant. She looked down to make sure her feet were on the floor. Yet her head felt like it was underwater, and if she tilted it to the side, maybe salt water would trickle from her ear.

Rita was careful to fit the top back on the plastic vial. She wanted the whole rest of her life to feel just like this. After remembering to open the bathroom door, she found the colorful patio and, with it, the blinding sun. Where was the flip-flop girl? She supposed it didn't matter. She watched a wispy cloud for a moment and then touched the worn tablecloth. So soft. And pink, like Easter eggs.

She looked up to find a woman in a hospital johnny, a woman Rita had cared for, a woman whose nose and lips and skin were seared off. MVA — fiery car crash.

"Rita!" the woman said. "Have you had these tortilla chips? They're to die for." Since the woman had no lips, Rita couldn't tell if she was smiling or not.

"Mrs. Townsley?" Rita closed her eyes and cursed herself for buying K from such a sketchy place. Bad trip. Very bad. But when she opened her eyes, she saw Leonard Brown sitting beside Mrs. Townsley.

"How are you, beautiful?" Leonard said. He was luckier. His meth lab had exploded and just got his torso, so his family could have an open casket.

"I—I'm confused," Rita replied. She turned to the next table, where she found little Zachary Kowalski, critically injured in a house fire caused by his own mother, who fell asleep while sucking on a cigarette. Old mattress. Poof. His face was gray and ashen.

"Rita, I want to build a dinosaur with Legos. Will you get me Legos?"

"Sure, sweetie, I'll try to find some." All the kid wanted were some fucking Legos, and Rita couldn't even do that for him. Inhalation injuries. He died while two of the residents bickered over his oxygen saturation and whether to put him in the hyperbaric chamber.

At the corner table was Ethan Walker, another MVA, who sat with his legs splayed despite the modesty required for a hospital gown. Not that he had much left to see with all that charred flesh.

Rita pulled the tablecloth from the nearest table and sank to the concrete floor, covering her head in orange fabric to make everything go away. She only saw orange shapes, all citrusy bright. Blood pounded in her ears so she concentrated on the rhythm of her own heartbeat: *lub*dub, *lub*dub. She felt a hand rub her back the way her mother used to do. Rita welcomed the human touch and relaxed the taut muscles of her back.

"Are you okay?" It was Nellie Fisher, accident in a chemical factory. Her skin was raw and melty. Rita had given her a little more morphine than what Dr. Ahmed recommended.

"I can apply the silver sulfadiazine cream," Rita said.

"Sometimes even caregivers need a rest," Nellie said. "It's okay to ask for help."

Did she really give money to a mutt? Legos. She needed to find Legos. And where was Cal?

Before her afternoon shift, Rita stepped into the locker room shower. She loved this ritual ablution, scrubbing herself of any germs she'd brought into the hospital with a stiff loofah, pushing hard enough to make her skin angry and red.

She was thinking about the man she'd met at a cocktail party. Charming, attractive enough, and, best of all, unmarried. They did a line of coke together in the hall closet. At some point, Rita began talking about nursing, and the guy flipped out when she mentioned the burn unit. He said, *I could never do something like that.*

Rita squeezed more soap onto the sponge. She thrived on challenges, craved the adrenaline rush of a code, and didn't even mind the heat. The nauseating smell bothered her for the first couple of weeks but that was years ago. She liked that she could handle the most gruesome wounds.

When she'd finished scrubbing, Rita twisted her hair into a bun and pulled a fresh pair of size medium scrubs from the stack. She wanted to check on Cal first, even before Melissa gave updates on their shared patients. But then Rita got stuck with a new admit and covered patients for Tanya while Tanya met with hospital counsel for an upcoming deposition.

Rita hurried into Cal's room, fully expecting a playful reprimand for being late. He stared at the TV, immersed in SportsCenter. Since he couldn't use his hands, he usually left it on ESPN. His dinner tray sat untouched.

"Javier didn't feed you?" Rita said, referring to one of the techs.

"I wanted you," he replied in a tiny voice as if he might cry.

"Well then, what's for dinner?" Rita smiled and hoped it didn't look too fake. She lifted the plastic cover from his plate.

"Salisbury steak," Cal said. "Which makes me wonder about the people of Salisbury. Why would they want to be associated with this jellied substance?"

"Didn't you ask for it?"

"I guess I was a little too optimistic when I ordered," he said. "But mashed potatoes are hard to fuck up. Let's start with those."

Rita dipped a spoon into the potatoes and held it near Cal's mouth. He leaned forward to take the bite, balancing his gauze mittens in the air. When they'd first done this, Rita had tried to put the food directly in his mouth, which they both agreed was ridiculous.

"Wrong again," he said. "It *is* possible to fuck up mashed potatoes."

"Milkshake?"

"Strawberry. No, chocolate."

"And fries. You need more calories," Rita scolded. "Your body's using a lot of energy trying to heal itself." She called nutrition services with the new order.

"I need the commode," Cal said after she'd hung up.

"Number one or number two?" If he had to urinate, she usually stayed in the room. Even though he always complained about having to pee sitting down like a girl.

"Numero uno."

After helping him to the commode—it was tricky getting out of bed without hands—she pulled the curtain around him and waited.

"Are you nervous about the skin grafting?" Rita asked.

"What's to be nervous about? The surgery will be done before your shift, so we won't miss any time together." The stream of urine stopped.

As Rita held his elbow for balance, he sighed. "Rita, do you have to wear so many clothes?"

"I'm afraid so." She pulled down his hospital johnny, which was still hiked up around his groin.

"Just a quick flash?" he said. "Please? Help a guy out."

Rita rolled her eyes but considered the request. "Cal, I'm not your stripper. And I wear this stuff for infection control."

"Sure. I know."

She felt guilty. It would certainly lift his spirits. Showing her breasts didn't seem like such a big deal.

"Rita, I can't even jerk myself off."

"I'm sorry," she said, with genuine contrition, and flicked the brim of his cap because she didn't know what else to do.

In Tijuana, Rita followed the zebra pulling a chariot. For a moment, she convinced herself that the magical zebra would lead her to the Legos. She watched her sandaled feet move and tried not to look at the faces. The last time Rita looked up, she saw the electrical burn guy—lightning strike—and felt deeply ashamed because she couldn't remember the man's name.

As they passed street vendors, Rita scanned the wares for Legos but most of the goods were gaudy sombreros, piñatas, or patterned blankets. A frog piñata blinked its bubble eyes. Left foot, right foot, left again. Follow the zebra.

A man with devil horns tossed fire sticks into the air. He twirled them so the flames spun into a giant fireball. It occurred to Rita that such a worldly man would know where to find Legos.

"*Señor,*" she said, "I need Legos. Where can I buy Legos?"

He whistled through his teeth and tossed a fire stick high above Rita. She jumped back but was undeterred.

"Legos," she demanded. "Do you understand?"

"Play catch," said the devil man. He threw a flaming baton at her. Rita instinctively covered her face. He caught it just as she felt the heat. A trick.

"Do you know how dangerous that is? Do you?"

The devil man laughed. Rita gave up on him. She would follow the zebra and chariot wherever it would take her. From behind, the chariot driver looked like Cal. Did Rita spread the bacteria to Cal? Or was it from the skin graft surgery? Another nurse? They were all responsible.

The zebra stopped by a fountain, its pool shimmering with coins. The bubbling water was cool and refreshing. Rita jumped in and scrubbed until her skin felt numb.

Before Cal went into septic shock and crashed, they watched the snow falling in wet clumps. His room had a nice aerial view of the courtyard. A blanket of snow covered the skeletal trees and children's playground.

"Rita," he said, "love me yet?"

She bent over his chilled body, tilted the brim of his cap, kissed his forehead. "Not quite yet."

"A kiss. I must be looking pretty bad." He laughed softly, probably because a real laugh would hurt too much. The skin grafts on his chest weren't healing well. "You know, you're the only one who hasn't asked what happened."

His burns were consistent with self-injury, despite his story about spilling kerosene on himself and standing too close to the ignition of the space heater. It was Rita's job to patch up his body, not his mind. She let the consulting psychiatrist bother Cal about the suicide attempt.

"Doesn't matter," she said.

"I tried to stop it," Cal said. "Because I changed my mind. Can't a person do that?"

"Of course." Rita checked the flow of intravenous cephalexin. Why was he telling her? She hadn't been worried about him until this sudden confession.

"I want to feel the snow," he said.

"I could bring some ice chips for you. We could have a mini snowball fight." She held the straw to his lips. "Water?"

"No thanks. Can we go outside?"

"You know you can't be exposed like that."

"What's it going to hurt?"

"My conscience. My professional reputation. Should I go on?" Rita was encouraged by his playful tone.

"I already have MRSA," Cal said, pronouncing it *mersa* just like the nurses. Lay people called it the superbug.

Rita pulled the privacy curtain around his bed.

"How about a peep show?" she whispered. It seemed like the least she could do.

Cal grinned.

"But no touching, okay?"

"I can't feel anything with these," he said, holding up his gauze mittens. "Never will."

And it was then that Rita's heart swelled with blood, engorged, and she felt as though her rib cage might crack open. She realized she'd been holding her breath.

Cal started humming the Billy Joel song: *We didn't start the fire / it was always burning / since the world's been turning.* She wanted to keep him in her bed, covered in blankets, and protect him from the world forever.

He gave up on Billy Joel and hummed the traditional striptease song, cueing Rita to start. She took off her gown and scrub top first. Rita twirled the shirt over her head several times before feeling ridiculous and collapsing with laughter. When she saw that his face was flushed red, she was embarrassed too.

"Well," Rita said.

Cal looked down at his mittens.

"You're fighting this infection, right?" she asked, folding her arms across her chest.

"Sure I am."

"Promise?"

"Yeah."

Rita turned so that her back faced Cal and pulled the scrub top over her head.

"Nothing I haven't seen before," he said.

"I know, stud." Despite the warmth, the skin on her arms prickled with goose bumps. She knew, somehow, that Cal wouldn't make it, but wrote off her intuition as bunk, and that weekend went hiking with friends. Thirty-six hours later, her coworkers Danielle and Javier had cleaned his body and were waiting for the morgue attendant.

While splashing in the fountain, Rita could still feel the germs crawling under her skin. They itched like tiny ants, scurrying up and down her arms, except inside the layers of her skin: the epidermis, dermis, and hypodermis. Skin—she knew skin and its behaviors well, the way it puckered and flaked, the way it smelled when singed.

And suddenly the flip-flop girl appeared in front of Rita.

"It's okay, it's me, Ashley," she said. "Let's get out of the water."

"But I feel them," Rita said. "I can feel the bacteria in my skin. Look." Rita pointed to the germs crawling on her forearm.

"We'll get the rest in the bathtub. Let's go home, okay?"

Yes, Rita thought, home. And before she could remember where home was, she let the girl hold her hand and lead her from the bubbling water.

Primal Son

OLIVIA'S BABY HAD ten long fingers and ten toes. The doctors said he was perfectly healthy despite the thick black hair that covered most of his body. His jaw jutted out and his nose was really just a pair of nostrils. The natural birthing process could temporarily distort facial features, they said, and sometimes babies were born with excess hair. His mental and physical development didn't seem to be affected. In fact, he scored a perfect ten on the Apgar.

When the nurse brought the baby to the maternity suite, Olivia asked if it was something genetic. The nurse smiled sweetly and announced, "Here is your son! I'll leave you alone so you can bond. Then we'll start lactation lessons."

Instead of joy, Olivia felt guilt. Not only had her body just been ripped apart, but this? What had she done to deserve this? Her husband, David, slept on the daddy cot. The maternity suite tried to look like a budget hotel room, complete with wood laminate nightstands, but the fluorescent lights revealed its true purpose. She tried to convince herself that the baby's body hair would fall out soon, like the doctors had assured her.

"David," she whispered. "Get up."

He rose, then stumbled to her side.

"Oh my God," he said.

Their son squirmed in the swaddling blanket, but never made a sound. Soft black hair swirled around his cheeks and forehead. The only exposed skin—around his eyes, nose, and lips—was pink and wrinkled.

"They took him away so fast," David said, "and he was covered in slime—I mean, your protective slime and blood and everything."

"Slime," she echoed.

"So—are you going to say it or should I?" David asked.

"Say what?"

"He looks like—" David started. "I can't."

"Do you think he's really ours?" Olivia asked.

"I watched everything. This little, um, primate came out of you."

Her breasts throbbed with every heartbeat. My son, she thought. Maybe if she said it enough times, it would be true. *My son, my son, my son.*

Olivia remembered his conception well. It was the night of the ice storm and they had lost electricity for an hour. In the candlelight, Olivia was staring at the daddy longlegs dancing across the ceiling, her knees pulled to her chest, held in a position to increase the chances of conception. After two miscarriages and three failed cycles of IVF, she knew all about chances. She knew about percentages and probabilities and bad luck. A wet tongue licked her cheek.

"Rufus," she said to their shelter terrier, sitting on the edge of the bed. "It's okay. I'm fine."

Neither of them had bothered to close the door, so Rufus had watched them the whole time, as if making sure David wasn't hurting Olivia. The dog's amber eyes followed her movements.

"Hey, Rufie," David said, rolling onto his wife. He balanced his upper body on her knees, arms outstretched. "Look! I'm Superman!"

"More like Jesus. Superman put his arms in front," said Olivia, glad that David could still be goofy during an act that had become a chore, but annoyed that he'd chosen the present moment to be playful. "I'm busy conceiving. You're not supposed to be on top anymore. I'm done with you."

"Oh, the agony," he said. "The moral weight of so many sinners."

"Off. I mean it." When he didn't respond, Olivia engaged Rufus. "Help me, Rufus, help me!"

The dog growled and snapped at David. Her husband called a truce and flopped onto his side of the bed, burrowing under the down comforter. On the nightstand, her orchid flaunted its purple bloom, brilliant in the candle's glow. Everything seemed to be fertile except Olivia.

"Maybe Rufus could get you pregnant," David said, with more sadness than contempt.

"Please don't start this."

"I've been thinking," he said. "Maybe we should consider international adoption."

They had agreed to try everything before talking about adoption. Olivia, not yet ready to have this conversation, resorted to parsing semantics: "Why not domestic adoption?"

"Because then our child will always know he's adopted. If we had a Mandarin baby, there would be no doubt. I hate it when couples try to pass it off like it's their own."

"*She*," Olivia corrected. "I thought they gave away the girls in China."

She put her knees down. Technology had failed them, so

she was making a final attempt the old-fashioned way. During the day, when she wasn't thinking about babies, she convinced people that technology was good. She convinced people with strokes and brain injuries to lie still in the MRI coffin, and hold still now, all in the name of research. Then she went back to the imaging lab and traced their brain structures on a computer.

"So you want to give up?" she said.

"You think that's giving up?" David said. He lay on his side, his back to her. "Having our child by adopting is giving up?"

"That's not what I'm saying."

"You're saying you want a white kid."

"No," Olivia said. "I don't care what it looks like. I want a child that has your laugh and my clumsiness and your double-jointed elbows. I want to feel it grow and kick inside me. Am I that selfish?"

"No," David said. "It's natural. You want to propagate the species. Fucking Darwin."

"Yeah. Fuck him." Olivia reached over and plucked the orchid flower, tucking it behind her ear.

Her newborn son wasn't interested in her breast, which added insult to injury. Olivia stroked his wrinkled little cheek to get him to suckle, but he kept turning his head away. The lactation coach told them to be patient because some babies took longer to latch on than others.

"He doesn't even like me," Olivia said, watching his glossy brown eyes.

"Give him some time," David said, revving up for a joke. "He just hasn't discovered the pleasures of the nipple yet."

Bingo. Olivia knew her husband well. "Maybe if you reasoned with him, he'd take an interest."

"Okay," David said. "We'll have a man-to-man talk. Or man-to—whatever."

"Well, don't let me get in the way." Olivia passed him to her husband, who had scooted onto the bed.

"Listen, little guy. This," David said, cupping her breast, "is heaven. You've got to trust me on this. If it were socially acceptable, I'd nurse too."

Suddenly Olivia was overwhelmed. Seeing David and their son together made her eyes well up. Maybe it was just a hormone surge, but it felt genuine.

"Look at that beautiful pinkness," David continued. "And it's all for you. Right there for the sucking. See?" He traced her nipple and now she was leaking everywhere.

"Hey," he said. "Are you crying?"

"Happy tears," said Olivia, choking back a sob.

Their son fell asleep. Olivia wanted him closer to her, even though her arms ached from holding him—she needed to feel him against her body. David passed him back to her as if the baby were made of porcelain and might crack if they weren't careful.

"What should we name him?" she asked. "I was a little superstitious before, but he's alive and well. We need a name."

"George. You know, like Curious George."

"That's not funny," Olivia said. The joke was so sharp, so hurtful, that she felt a little piece of her heart tissue die. Just like that.

"I thought you wanted William for a boy," said David.

"He doesn't exactly look like a William, does he?" Of this she was certain. His name wasn't William. He was her son, her baby, her everything. Who could put a name on that?

David, always wanting the last word, said, "I'm not sure *what* he looks like."

Upon their leaving the hospital, the birth certificate read BABY BOY JENSEN. Olivia and David had bought a car seat, fitted by a specialist, and their son was strapped safely inside. But the outside world still seemed threatening.

"Drive slower," Olivia said.

"I am. Calm down," said David, without his usual humor.

A little hybrid car cut them off. David gave it the finger.

"Jesus," he said. "Don't they know we have a newborn here?"

"Maybe we can get him a helmet. Traumatic brain injury is so scary, especially the developmental cases," Olivia said, twisting toward the backseat. She could swear her infant son was reaching for her and she couldn't stand not holding him.

"I think we can handle this without a goddamn helmet."

"But sometimes it's just an accident," said Olivia, already afraid of losing what, in just forty-eight hours, had become essential to her.

"Wait a minute, Dr. Jensen. You're still a scientist, right? Searching for reasonable explanations? Or have the mommy hormones taken over?"

"I have stitches and I'm wearing mesh undies. Don't be an asshole," she said.

"Don't say asshole in front of him," David said. He took the corner with caution.

"You just did, asshole."

"We're going to be awesome parents, aren't we?"

Olivia was now responsible for another—*she* would be a great parent. She vowed then to do anything for her son.

When they arrived home, David's mother, Margaret, was cleaning the kitchen, wearing bright yellow gloves and a look of determination. In the last weeks of her pregnancy, Olivia left half-empty mugs of herbal tea and damp tea bags on every surface. The mugs left a constellation of dark rings, incomplete circles, and crescent moons on the countertop. Margaret threw a dish towel over her shoulder.

"Why hello, Mommy and Daddy!" she said. "And where is my grandson?"

"Here," David said. "Hi, Mom." Because Olivia was still sore, David carried the car seat and guest of honor. Margaret and Rufus approached at the same time. The dog seemed puzzled by the little squirming thing and sniffed the entire car seat.

"My," Margaret said. "He still has that thick hair. It usually falls out."

"Aren't his brown eyes gorgeous?" Olivia adjusted the knit cap he kept taking off. She wished it would cover more of his face, protect him from the people staring.

"Welcome home, my little grandson," Margaret said. She leaned in, and he wrapped his fist around her gloved finger. "Did you decide on a name?"

"Not yet," said David.

Margaret was touching him with gloves, a detail not lost on Olivia. Her mother-in-law had held him briefly in the hospital, and only as he slept.

"Well," Margaret said. "You both must be exhausted. Are you hungry? I made lasagna and shepherd's pie. All the extra is labeled in the freezer."

"Sure. I'll eat," said David. Olivia couldn't fathom how David could think of food when their son hadn't eaten in hours.

"I'm going to try and feed him." Olivia lifted her son from the car seat. She then retreated to the living room and sat in the rocking chair they'd bought specially for nursing. Now the ergonomic chair seemed trivial, the least of her worries.

She adjusted her breastfeeding poncho to reveal her naked

chest. He still wouldn't latch on. At the hospital, the lactation coach told her to keep trying and supplement with formula. Her breasts felt as though they might rupture, bursting with nutrition for the baby who refused it.

"Oh, sweetie," Olivia said. "What's wrong? Please eat."

He watched her face with those sweet brown eyes. Rufus interrupted by sniffing Olivia's arms and hands. Then he investigated the baby, pressing his nose to the blanket.

"How's everything going?" Margaret said from the hallway.

"He doesn't want me."

"Did you tickle his lips and cheeks?" Margaret said. "Is his belly pressed to yours?"

Clearly this was a problem her mother-in-law could tackle, unlike the baby's appearance. Olivia grew frustrated. Margaret now hovered over them, as if her presence alone would help.

"It's okay, really," Olivia said, wanting some privacy. "The two of us have to figure this out."

"Oh," Margaret said. "Then I'll get the laundry from the dryer."

"Thank you," Olivia said, but her mother-in-law was already gone.

The day she'd passed twelve weeks, the vulnerable first trimester, Olivia returned home to a Szechuan feast. David was an excellent cook and she was convinced he'd be a great stay-at-home dad. They'd started the paperwork to adopt a Chinese girl, and since Olivia had suffered two miscarriages before, she didn't want to tell David of the pregnancy until she was thirteen weeks along.

"*Ni hao*," David said. He stirred sizzling vegetables with a wooden spoon.

"What?" Olivia was so disoriented, and eager to share the news, that she didn't recognize the greeting.

"It's 'hello' in Mandarin. Literally, 'you good,'" he said. "I got CDs from the public library."

"David," she said. "Sit down."

"What happened? Did the lab lose funding?"

"We don't need the Mandarin CDs." Olivia rubbed her belly, a gesture she found clichéd but entirely appropriate for the situation.

"Are you sure? Have you seen Dr. Garrett without me?"

"Yes," she said, smiling. "Almost thirteen weeks."

"Oh my God," he said, dropping to his knees. He pressed his head against her abdomen. "I can feel it. Swimming around inside. I swear, I can feel it."

"Come on." She laughed.

They slow danced around the dining room without music. David knocked over a chair in his excitement and dipped her low. They kissed, giggling. Rufus barked. The stir-fry began to smoke and they didn't care.

They called him B.B. for now, short for Baby Boy. Margaret left after she'd cleaned the whole house, and David was out getting diapers. Olivia and B.B. rocked in the ergonomic chair. She didn't want to invite friends over. Although many of her friends were scientists, they were still human, and she was afraid of their reactions.

"B.B.," she said. "Do you want to hear a lullaby?"

He stared at her. He still didn't cry, but he grunted sometimes.

"Do I even know any lullabies? 'Rock-a-Bye Baby.' But that's boring. How does that Cat Stevens song go? *I'm being followed by a moonshadow*—"

Rufus trotted to the door and did his special stranger bark, which put Olivia on alert.

"Who's there?" she yelled, hoping she wouldn't upset B.B.

"It's just me," David answered, his voice muffled as he unlocked the door, all the while wearing an ape costume. "Rufus, it's okay man, calm down."

Olivia pulled B.B. closer to her body: "What the fuck are you *doing?*"

"No more swearing," David said. "Not in front of the kid."

"Well, you didn't answer my fucking question."

The monkey suit was hideous. The dark fur was matted down in random places and the face was shiny black plastic. The hands and chest were slick vinyl or some other equally horrible synthetic material. Rufus had retreated to the corner of the living room, growling every so often.

"It's so we can bond with our son," David said, his voice breaking.

"I'm sorry, honey," Olivia said, wanting to take back her obvious display of contempt. It wasn't as though her methods were working.

David leaned in and B.B. whined, a high-pitched squeal. B.B. clutched David's fake fur and clung to his chest.

"There's my little boy," David cooed. "You just stick with your daddy."

Olivia had never seen B.B. so happy. His squeals of joy alternated with panting breaths.

"I was thinking we could make another costume and cut holes for your nipples," said David. "I bought a bunch of fabric too."

B.B. seemed content now in his father's furry arms, settling into a calmer rhythm.

David continued: "We made this little guy. What if we're

killing him? Do you know what we're doing? We're not trying to kill him but what if we do? We're responsible. For everything."

"Let's take things one at a time," Olivia said. "I'm going to cut some of the fabric and make a fur blanket, okay? You stay here with him."

Olivia unfolded the fake fur on the kitchen table and cut a neat square without measuring. It was nice to be away from B.B. for a few minutes, but she felt incomplete without him. When she returned to the living room, they all sat on the sofa. David held him, swaddling him in the fur blanket, and Olivia leaned over to offer her breast. B.B. latched on right away. She felt immediate relief. *My son, my son, my son.*

Every couple of hours, B.B. would indicate his hunger by emitting several high-pitched shrieks, and then he would purse his lips. He'd nurse as long as he had his little patch of fur to grip in one hand and could knead it with his fingers. Because it was so much easier, Olivia preferred to be topless. Otherwise B.B. would tear her shirt to get to her breast. And the breastfeeding poncho seemed ridiculous in its modesty.

Olivia learned to sleep when he did. Instead of using the crib they'd carefully assembled weeks before his birth, Olivia placed him beside her on the queen bed. She was aware of the experts who frowned upon cosleeping, but she'd no more roll onto her child than cut off her own leg—he was still attached, part of her body. And this way, even when she drifted into twilight sleep, he could get sustenance.

When he was awake, B.B. had the habit of clinging to Olivia, wrapping his flexible legs and arms around her waist. At first she was disconcerted by the ease with which he could hold on, and also by the bruises that appeared on her torso from his little hands and feet pinching her skin, but she became accustomed to it. She liked to have her hands free to do household chores. For example, Olivia could make the coffee for David and her own decaf green tea, plus she could prepare the morning meal to her liking. She'd been craving sugar constantly and David always made savory foods like omelets or bacon.

Several mornings later—it could've been a week, because time didn't mean much these days—Olivia was making her breakfast. As she spread Nutella on her toaster waffles, David entered the kitchen wearing the ape costume.

"Jesus, David," she said. "Warn me next time."

B.B., having had his fill of breast milk, squealed and then jumped from Olivia to his father. She knew it wasn't safe, and that she shouldn't encourage the behavior, but he had a remarkable sense of balance. She also knew that David was feeling left out.

"Yeah!" David yelled. "Who's your daddy?"

Olivia licked the spoon. The hazelnut chocolate oozed on her tongue. Bliss. For a moment, she could almost forget that her son was abnormal. The only thing that could make this Nutella waffle better was whipped cream. Maybe a sprinkle of cinnamon.

Rufus waited patiently at her feet for any leftovers or crumbs. He'd been tolerating the newest member of the family and now accepted table scraps in lieu of attention. Lately he spent most of his time in the backyard, digging holes under the flower beds.

As she watched B.B. crawl over David, she tried to get a sense of herself without her son. It felt wrong, like starting with the left foot as she climbed the stairs. Even as she approached her husband and son, she was ashamed of what she was about to do.

She mimicked B.B.'s shriek. He immediately jumped back

to her. It only seemed fair that he preferred Olivia, since her body had done most of the work to make his. And her body continued to do most of the work. David's only job was to keep them flush with groceries and diapers.

"Come on," David protested.

"Meh," Olivia said, shrugging. B.B. snuggled into her shoulder.

David took a different tack. "I was thinking," he said, his voice muffled by the costume's mask.

"Mmm?" Olivia didn't put quite enough butter between the waffle and the Nutella.

"You should probably wear a robe or something. What if there's someone looking through the windows?"

The thought of anyone wanting to see her nursing was so absurd that Olivia snorted, a few drops of urine bursting from her bladder. B.B. began his squeal-pant, which approximated a giggle.

"So," Olivia said, "you think a peeping Tom wants to see my boobs feeding my infant son, all *National Geographic*–style?"

"You haven't worn a shirt in the last five days," David replied.

"You do realize you're wearing an ape suit?" Olivia said, crunching into the next waffle.

"Mom's coming over at ten thirty. She wants to see him." David made a grunting sound and motioned for B.B. Then David took B.B.'s hands and swung them in the air. B.B., delighted, did his squeal-pant again. Olivia did like to see her son happy.

She went to the fridge—she was still ravenous—and retrieved a box of blueberries and a Tupperware of sliced mango. "Margaret can come over. But I'm not putting a shirt on."

• • •

By the time Margaret arrived, B.B. had had another feeding and Olivia devoured the last of the strawberries. Margaret let herself in and found the two of them on the sofa, swaying as Olivia hummed "Moonshadow." Olivia could swear that her mother-in-law blushed at the sight of her breasts. Or maybe the bruises.

"Hi, Mom," David said, appearing in the kitchen doorway.

Margaret yelped, letting her Macy's bag drop to the floor. Then she smoothed the tails of her linen blouse and patted her hair. "I don't find this joke very funny."

"It's not a joke," said David. "You want some coffee?"

Margaret declined. "It's not some kind of—of perversion?"

"Just watch." David grunted to B.B., who eagerly crawled into his father's arms.

"He was almost asleep," Olivia snarled.

David swung B.B. toward the ceiling. Of course B.B. was excited and showed it with his version of giggling. Olivia knew he wanted to go even higher. *Weeeeeeeee!* he seemed to be saying.

Margaret asked if she could hold him. But B.B. squirmed from her arms, always returning to either Olivia or David. Margaret tried three times before giving up. She then revealed the contents of the Macy's bag, an assortment of boy-themed onesies that B.B. would just tear off.

"Maybe we could go for a walk?" Margaret suggested. It was, in her words, "a beautiful October day." She'd bought them a fancy European stroller before B.B. was born and wanted to make use of it.

This should be good, Olivia thought—there's no way B.B. would stay in a stroller. She turned out to be right, and they had to scrap the stroller because he kept leaping out of it. Olivia wore the nursing poncho, and since B.B. insisted on skin-to-skin contact, he stayed underneath. Margaret, for her part, insisted that David take off the monkey costume. B.B. wanted nothing to do with hairless David or Margaret.

The three of them (four, counting B.B.) had gotten about a block before a neighborhood woman in a blue tracksuit and sheltie approached them. Olivia didn't know the woman's name, but she was kind and always gave Rufus a bacon treat. Trixie, that was the sheltie's name.

"Oh, is it the new baby?" the woman said, pointing toward the squirming mass under Olivia's poncho.

Olivia pulled back the fabric. B.B. thrust an arm outward. The woman stepped back.

"His—his eyes," she stammered. "His brown eyes are beautiful."

"Aren't they gorgeous?" Margaret chimed.

Olivia could feel the woman's gaze on her naked torso. B.B. started to whine and purse his lips for her breast.

"Those bruises," the woman said, and looked suspiciously at David.

"The bruises," Olivia said, now enraged, "are none of your fucking business."

"Whoa, mama wolf," said David, which only angered Olivia more.

"Who's hungry for lunch?" said Margaret as she righted the poncho, covering B.B. back up.

Olivia didn't want to explain her condition or her son's condition. She didn't want to explain his existence. She wrapped her arms around him and returned to the house without looking back.

Olivia decided to make a costume for herself. She was afraid of going to the doctor for her postpartum checkup, all covered in bruises, and having some intern accuse her husband of abuse. She had to sew the costume by hand because she didn't want to explain to her friend Anjali why she needed to borrow a sewing machine.

"This is not normal," David said, referring to B.B.'s once-novel leaps and sense of balance. From David's shoulder, B.B. watched the needle disappear into the brown fabric.

"You think I don't know that? What the fuck do you want me to do?"

"We have to get him in for a two-week checkup," David said. They'd had an appointment scheduled for that day, but Olivia had refused to go. And David had been wearing normal clothes, so B.B. wouldn't touch him. David had changed into his costume to restore the peace.

"Doctors are pseudo-scientists," Olivia said, trying to explain her thought process and make even stitches at the same time. "They'll take photos of him and write up a case study and publish it in the *Journal of Genetic Freaks.*"

Olivia then realized that she couldn't go to her own postpartum appointment without the baby — wouldn't that be just as suspicious? She liked the almost meditative process of making the costume and decided to finish it anyway. It would be winter in a few short weeks, and both she and B.B. would appreciate the extra warmth.

"Look," David said. "I think he has double-jointed elbows."

B.B. reached for the floor lamp, swung his body to it. Everything crashed to the ground when he realized it was hot. Olivia scooped him up. He seemed to be unfazed.

"It's okay, B.B. You're such a brave boy, I know," she said.

"What a brave boy," David said, stroking his forehead. The three of them formed a tight triumvirate. Thankfully, their son was fine.

"You know the pictures, right?" Olivia said. "In the genetics literature, those pictures of naked kids with black bars across their eyes?"

"I know. They're awful," David said. "But we can't stay holed up here forever."

"Let's go somewhere no one knows us." B.B. wasn't thriving in this environment. That's exactly what they needed, she thought.

Olivia was almost finished with her costume, just a few alterations left. David was on hold with the travel website, scratching his fake fur and watching B.B. climb from the sofa and up the bookcase. They were also having issues with B.B.'s passport, since they hadn't changed his birth certificate.

"Okay," David said into the phone. "Yes. Flight to Dar es Salaam and Kigoma. Two weeks at the Gombe Forest Lodge. Right."

They'd decided on Tanzania, partly because they didn't know anyone there, but also because the national parks had untouched jungles where B.B. could play freely. They'd learned that Tanzania had thriving primate populations, some habituated to humans.

Olivia hummed, looking up from her sewing every few moments to check on B.B. He was a wonderful acrobat, swinging and climbing and sailing through the air. Sometimes he fell but he jumped up again. His bones were still soft, Olivia reasoned.

"We're all set for next week," David told her. "Are we crazy to take a baby on a plane?"

Olivia shrugged. "Anjali put a little brandy in her daughter's bottle when they flew to India. Did you book the kennel for Rufus?"

B.B. crawled over David and examined the ears of the monkey suit. They looked just like human ears, maybe a little bigger. Ever curious, B.B. stuck his finger inside.

Olivia set down her sewing for a moment and started in

on a bowl of raspberries. B.B. examined David's fur, getting down to the skin of the costume.

"What if," he said, "what if we did something wrong? Remember when you had that drink of Champagne at Kevin's party?"

"It was a sip. Don't be fucking ridiculous."

"I've got it. The week before he was born, remember? We made love in the nursery —"

"He's fine the way he is!" Olivia wanted to hold B.B. and protect him from the world. She curled up with her son and husband on the sofa. B.B. squirmed through them. He scaled the back of the sofa, leaped upward, and hung from the curtain rod.

If another environment might be better for her son, she owed it to him to explore the possibility. Quite simply, she would do whatever it took to make her son happy.

In the end, Olivia gave him formula laced with brandy and wrapped him in a thick blanket. He was upset to see David without the costume so they added a little more brandy. At the airport, they got through security easier than expected. People stared, some pointed, and a few giggled. Maybe Olivia should've had some brandy too. The hours on the plane seemed like days. She wore a loose tank top, sans bra, and the breastfeeding poncho. Underneath, she could feel B.B.'s breath, slow and even.

"He's zonked," David said, peeking under the poncho.

In another version of her life, Olivia might worry about the alcohol killing her son's developing neurons. Now, given her greater concerns, she found this laughable.

"Just think," David said. "Soon he'll get to play outside."

Olivia busied herself by coloring all the little squares in the *TravelPost* crossword puzzle black, keeping her left hand on her slumbering son. The plane was so small, a metal bird hurtling through space. Little bird in the great big sky, she thought, please get us there safely.

To Olivia's relief, they arrived at the scheduled time. B.B. still seemed drowsy, not yet interested in his new surroundings. They boarded a ferry to take them across the lake to the Gombe Forest Lodge. Thankfully, Olivia could keep her dozing son covered with the poncho fabric, away from the prying eyes of the captain. The ride took more than an hour, and with the gentle waves, Olivia nodded off.

Their deluxe tent had rich textures — crisp white sheets, soft woven pillow covers, smooth wooden masks, and rough-hewn supports. A canopy of mosquito netting floated above the bed. No doubt B.B. would try to climb it. Olivia took off her poncho and tank top, then surveyed the room for sharp edges, with B.B. rustling in her arms. The tent opened to a private deck, giving them a spectacular view of the dense forest. Sunlight penetrated the canopy of trees and made the leaves shimmer. In the distance, through a copse of smaller trees, Olivia caught a glimpse of the shore.

"Look at all the trees, B.B.!"

B.B. squealed and wriggled in excitement. David soon joined them, dressed in the monkey suit. B.B. leaped onto his father's shoulder for a higher vantage point.

"Wow," David said.

"Amazing, isn't it?" Olivia wondered aloud.

"Very."

The three of them stepped onto the veranda, the air warm and moist. A bird squawked at them like the neighborhood gossip. Everything was green, lush, alive. They sat, legs dangling from the edge. But B.B. burrowed into David as if he were afraid.

"Hey now," David said. "We thought you'd like it out here."

"It's okay, B.B. We can play later," Olivia added.

Something rustled in the distance, and she saw a flash of spotted fur among the foliage. As a leopard sauntered into view, Olivia held her breath. Of course B.B. sensed the leopard before they did—maybe B.B. had knowledge to impart. Her son the teacher. The beast came within twenty feet, passing them on its way to the lake for a long drink.

They waited an hour before exploring the lakeshore. With B.B. relaxed, they felt it was safe to venture out. He splashed in the cool water, dousing Olivia, happy as can be. David joined the game, and in seconds, they were all wet and laughing.

"I could stay here for a long time," Olivia said, wiping the water from her eyes.

"Yeah," David agreed. "It's pretty great." He picked a shiny water bug from Olivia's back.

Olivia's mate was grooming her. She giggled and couldn't deny that she was enjoying herself. She was amazed that it had taken a transatlantic flight, not to mention a difficult few weeks with B.B., to recognize what made her happy. She scooped up B.B. and they found a patch of sun to dry themselves and doze away the afternoon.

Eventually Olivia decided to put on her homemade costume. David and B.B. were on the veranda, trying to catch one of the darting lizards. She stepped into her furry creation, which was surprisingly comfortable, fit perfectly, and allowed her to move with ease—it almost melted into her skin. To be more authentic, she got on all fours and walked outside to greet her family. Now she actually looked like David's mate.

B.B. copied her, squealing with delight. She walked faster this way, closer to the ground, closer to her son. He climbed on her back. She liked this position, where she could see potential threats and feel that he was safe, right on top of her.

She jumped from the veranda into the bushes and motioned for David to follow them. *Come.* Suddenly she was famished. She wanted fruit, something succulent, fresh from the branch. They would have to go deeper into the jungle.

She grunted. Among the flora, she saw a hint of bright scarlet. The round fruit was ripe and heavy, hanging from the tree. Her mate grabbed it, took a bite, then handed it to her. She finished it, saving a piece of the soft flesh for her son. He ate it from her fingers and they all went deeper into the lush foliage.

Ex-Utero

DURING THE FIRST night of my surgery rotation, we lose electricity in a brilliant thunderstorm. The generator powers our essential equipment and every third fluorescent light. It's cozier somehow. I don't know if I should grab a chart or stay out of the way, so I pour lukewarm coffee and hover near the ambulance bay, watching the lightning crackle across the sky. Sheets of rain pelt the sliding glass doors, which no longer operate, and the rare soul who enters through the side door makes puddles on the gray-speckled linoleum.

My twenty-four-hour shift started at 6:30 that morning. After a cursory orientation, I spent most of the day avoiding the surgeons. They plunge scalpels into flesh, thriving on testosterone and stress hormones. They're at the top of the hospital hierarchy but I don't care for their arrogance. Since the surgical service is slow tonight, they sent me to the emergency department, otherwise known as the Pit, to learn how to suture.

"You," says Dr. Mehta, a third-year resident who told me to call him Sanjay, "get a history on Curtain 4. Police brought her in." He hands me the chart for Jane Doe. There's no chief complaint listed.

"Does she need sutures?" I ask.

"You tell me," he says, shoving his pen into the pocket of his white coat before spinning on the heel of his Nike.

"Right," I say, mustering some fake confidence before approaching my patient. I button the front of my waist-length white coat—that's how you can spot a med student, the shorter coats—and I'm thankful to be wearing comfortable scrubs rather than a skirt or slacks. Still, I wonder just how professional I could possibly look, with every available pocket filled to capacity: extra squares of gauze, a hemostat or two, a suture kit. But mainly my pockets are jammed with mini-guides on everything from drug dosages to common protocols—I feel better with this information on my person, this armor to deflect diagnostic bullets coming my way. My cell phone is also tucked in a pocket somewhere, not that anyone has service. We assume it's from the weather, which meteorologists are hyping as the storm of the century.

I really hope my Jane Doe isn't pregnant, because I haven't done my OB-GYN rotation yet. There's a rumor from upstairs that all the babies delivered on this shift have been stillborn. Not that I believe the nurses' rumors.

When I pull back the curtain, I find a middle-aged woman wrapped in a towel, her wrists bound by padded restraints. She weeps gray tears, the color of ash, mascara running down her cheeks like hot wax from a candle.

"I'm Zoe, a student doctor. What brings you here tonight?" I ask, although it's obvious she didn't come here willingly.

"No English," she says, then speaks in a sweet, lilting language—Farsi, or Hindi, or even Urdu—I have no idea. She motions for a pen and paper. I offer my personal notepad, the one with lists of drug dosages and silly mnemonic devices like "My Big Nob Vibrates Gently In Her Purulent Pelvis" to remember all the symptoms of renal failure.

The weeping woman struggles with the restraints so I hold the notepad for her. She makes a sketch of the earth and draws a giant X over it, retracing the X until she makes a hole in the paper. Her face twists, then hangs slack like a dry washcloth. She's given up.

Last year, this would've broken my heart. But I've witnessed enough heartbreaking scenes that they're starting to blur together. I've also seen—and experienced—the emotional fallout from caring too much. I still have nightmares about Ben, the ICU patient whose family had disowned him. Dying of pneumonia, secondary to late-stage AIDS, he begged me to stay with him. When he had to make a decision about whether he'd like to be resuscitated, he deferred to my "expertise." The agonal respirations were the worst, the croaking last gasps of a man I'd grown to care about. After he died, I had one session with a grief counselor but didn't have time to go back.

There must be something I can do for this poor woman in restraints. The skin around her wrists burns red, so I find a jar of Vaseline and rub a little on my own skin to show her what I'm doing. She allows me to take her hand and smooth the thick jelly where the restraints have chafed her.

"Better?" I say. My gesture seems trivial, but she murmurs and nods.

Someone has anticipated our communication problems, because one of the housekeepers stands at the foot of the bed and announces she's the translator.

"She wants to know if you're ready," says the housekeeper.

"Of course," I say. "I'd like to get started on her medical history."

"No. She wants to know if you're ready for the end of time."

"Not really," I say, noting her delusion. "I've been a little preoccupied. Can you tell me her name?"

The housekeeper consults my patient. They speak animatedly, with their hands for emphasis. I don't know why this woman is distressed, so I can't help her. I try to put myself in her position, scared and misunderstood and tied to a bed, but it's beyond the boundaries of my experience, like a foreign city I can imagine but have never visited.

"Her name," I repeat.

"What does it matter?" the housekeeper says. "Names aren't important anymore."

I underline Jane Doe on her chart, and when I present to Dr. Mehta, I'll suggest a psych consult. Any number of diagnoses seems plausible, and I haven't even gotten to the mental status questions. "Birth date?"

More chatting.

"It doesn't translate to the Western calendar. She wants you to help her warn everyone about the end."

I'm not sure what to do with this information, so I smile. Dr. Mehta is going to think I'm completely incompetent. If the situation weren't so absurd, I'd be more upset. Thankfully, Mehta isn't grading me — the surgeons are.

"This isn't funny," the housekeeper says. "She's dead serious."

My next patient is a forty-one-year-old male with a nasty scalp laceration above his temple. The surgical resident, who's supposed to be supervising my work, told me to sew him up. No staples because I needed to learn. I observed the suture technique earlier in the day, but I've never pierced a curved needle through living skin. Cadavers can't feel anything. My very alive patient will have more than three million pain receptors throughout his body.

I find the treatment room flooded in light. Krista, a veteran nurse and one of the few ED staff who bothered to introduce herself, has started rinsing the wound. The patient calmly endures the cleaning. The bloody water drips down the side of his head.

"Gown and gloves," Krista says.

I put on a yellow gown and latex gloves. She hands me a 50 cc syringe full of saline and tells me to irrigate. And keep irrigating until she gets back.

"Am I hurting you?" I ask the patient.

"No, not really," he says. I know he's lying. I try to be gentle, but it has to hurt. I marvel at the fact that I'm inflicting more pain in order to heal him, and this man trusts me.

"Did you get caught in the weather?" I ask.

"Yeah. Heck of a storm, but not the apocalypse they're calling it. You run all this on generators?" He looks at the halogen lamp positioned just above his head.

"Yes, I believe so."

Krista returns, instructing me to clip the hair around the wound and rinse with more sterile saline. I do exactly as she says. The gash is fully visible now, a red gorge of blood. The skin of his scalp is thin and pale as cigarette paper. I replace my gloves with a fresh pair.

Krista sets the cloth-wrapped suture tray on the stand beside me and unfolds the four points of the blue wrap. I carefully align the laceration under the opening in the sterile drape. His eyelashes flutter when the hem falls over the bridge of his nose.

"It's okay," he says. "Don't worry about me."

"I *am* worried about you," I say, adjusting the drape so he can see again. "That's my job."

"It's not to fix Humpty Dumpty?"

"Well, that too. Lidocaine?" I say, turning to Krista.

"Was that a question or a request?"

"Lidocaine," I say. "One percent."

She wipes the top of the bottle with an alcohol swab and plunges the syringe inside, drawing several cc's of the local anesthetic.

"This is going to hurt a little," I tell my patient.

"I've been hurt by women before," he says, laughing.

Krista gives me the syringe. I've only done sutures on bananas and cadavers, so my gloved hands are shaking when I inject the lidocaine. The skin around the wound swells. I do several injections to make sure it's sufficiently numb. I don't want him to feel my mistakes. I didn't learn how to sew until medical school, and I'm always surprised how difficult it is, holding the needle driver in my right hand and pick-ups, otherwise known as forceps, in my left. I'll start in the middle of the wound and line up the edges, then bisect it, as I've been taught.

"May I ask what happened here?" I say, gliding the needle through his scalp. I feel resistance but the needle is sharp. I pull the suture thread until it makes a little tent of skin. Too much. I can't help but shudder.

"What happened is I'm a klutz. Always hurting myself — typical leftie. This time I fell down the stairs."

"That must've hurt," I say, one suture complete. I'm determined to put this man back together. "You're lucky you didn't break anything."

"This is nothing. A month ago, I broke a couple of ribs when I fell off a horse. This time my scalp kept bleeding so I thought I should see a doctor."

"Did anyone look?" I ask, concentrating on the next stitch. It's crooked. "I mean, did anyone look at those ribs?"

"Nah. They were probably just bruised anyway."

"Painful?"

"Not so bad."

The last suture is neat and tight, but not so tight that the delicate skin puckers. I cut the excess from the knot, studying my handiwork. Krista whirls past and tells me nice job. I hadn't even noticed her absence. I wonder if the nurses get tired of babysitting the med students. Doctors make the decisions, but nurses run the place by doing all the dirty work.

"All done," I say. "You'll have to come back in a week to have the stitches taken out. Just wait here and I'll find someone to sign you out."

"Thank you, Doctor."

"You're welcome," I say, not bothering to correct him. I knew how to help this man. I'm proud of my sutures and thankful for the small victory. Then I remember I'd forgotten to give him a tetanus shot.

While I'm searching for Dr. Mehta, a woman in a wet trench coat flags me down. She looks confused.

"I'm looking for Mike Harper," she says. "His head was bleeding?"

"Right. He's over in Curtain 2, doing just fine. Are you family?"

"His wife."

"We had to put in a few stitches. Do you know if he's had a recent tetanus? We should probably give him a booster." I don't think she's listening to me. She's already at his side, clutching his arm to her breast, his hand over her heart.

"I'm sorry, baby," she says in a way that seems rehearsed. "I'm so sorry. It was an accident. A misunderstanding."

"I know, hon, I know." He glances at me.

"We need to get a tetanus for you, Mr. Harper," I say. "Just sit tight."

"I've been waiting over an hour. I'll just see my family doctor tomorrow morning."

"Five minutes," I say, hoping I can get a social worker down here that quickly. If I'd taken the time to put myself in his wet tennis shoes, to truly empathize, I would've seen the warning signs. It all makes sense now. People who fall have scrapes on their hands from trying to catch themselves.

I prepare my presentation for Dr. Mehta. He seemed relatively subdued when I'd presented Jane Doe, but that was only because he was in a hurry. Most residents and faculty prefer the Socratic method of instruction, otherwise known as a form of public humiliation called pimping. The goal is to ask difficult questions you know the student can't answer. And embarrass her in front of the group.

The method seems particularly cruel to inflict on sleep-deprived overachievers, we academically gifted students who aren't used to being wrong. Ever. That's how we got into med school in the first place. Instead of cooperative learning, we have to endure this macho posturing like the generations before us.

The first time, I cried. During my internal medicine rotation, I couldn't remember the last symptom of renal failure—my mind went blank. I had failed. The tears burned in my eyes. From then on, my team knew me as the Girl Who Cried. And I'd lost what little respect I had to start with.

Any strong emotion used to trigger the waterworks. Especially frustration. When I was young and learning the violin, if I didn't play the song perfectly after the first few times, I'd let the tears drip down my cheeks, onto the chin rest, as I continued to practice the song by memory. In college, I had a special stall in the women's bathroom on the fourth floor of the chemistry building, where I'd go to cry after we received our exam scores. Now, though, I'd learned to control it by biting the inside of my cheek until it bled or until I could see swirls in my peripheral vision.

I take a deep breath and steel myself for the encounter with Dr. Mehta. Fortunately, in the ED, we mostly work one-on-one. There's no group for Mehta to haze me in front of, like on the medicine rounds. Plus, I'd done a good job on Mr. Harper's sutures, and he's in an abusive relationship—he needs me as an advocate. As I'm looking up the number for social work, I see Mr. Harper and his wife go off into the storm, leaving against medical advice.

I don't have time to ruminate because Mehta grabs my arm and leads me toward Curtain 6. He says I'll want to see this. Nate, a fellow student I dated for several months, follows on our heels. He's rotating in OB, so he must be doing a consult.

"This is one for the journals," he whispers. "Complained of abdominal pain so they did a CT to rule out appendicitis."

"I thought you were on the mommy squad."

"I am. Team Vagina all the way," Nate says. "But they found something *very* interesting on the CT."

"What's the most common cause of sexual ambiguity?" Mehta barks at me.

I feel stupid because I have no idea.

"Congenital adrenal hyperplasia," Nate offers.

"How did you know that?" I hiss at him through my teeth.

"Very good, Nate," says Mehta, and I'm immediately jealous that he knows Nate's name and not mine. "Too bad that's not our diagnosis."

"I did some reading," Nate whispered.

The three of us approach a young man, maybe twenty-something, curled on the exam table. Another guy sits on the floor cross-legged, picking a guitar. He plays a melancholy flamenco tune with his long fingers. The patient fidgets with his hospital johnny, unties the neck and rolls it down. Under the gown, his chest is decorated in tattoo art, vines and skulls and gothic script. A dark serpent slithers up his left biceps.

"Can you give me some drugs or something?" the young man asks.

"Not until we figure out what's going on. Nate," says Mehta, "please escort this talented musician to the waiting area."

"He can stay," the young man says, squirming on the table and making the paper crinkle. "He's my entertainment. Any requests?"

"I have some news that may be disturbing," says Dr. Mehta.

"Hepatitis? Or the big C?"

"We found a mass in your abdomen. More specifically, in your lower abdomen."

"Dude, that sounds serious," the guitarist says. "Can I have your Ramírez if you don't make it?" He strums the melody to "Amazing Grace." Nate's scribbling on his notepad. I wonder if he got to examine the patient. In any case, I can't figure out why someone from OB is even here.

"I don't think it's malignant," Dr. Mehta replies. "Are you—"

"You don't *think* it's cancer? Or you know it's *not* cancer?" the young man says.

"Are you aware that you have elevated levels of several steroid precursors?" Dr. Mehta says.

"Like 'roids? No way."

"We've done some tests and found significant levels of estrogen and progesterone, among others," Dr. Mehta says. "Just to confirm: you're not taking *any* medications or supplements?"

"No. I've told you three fucking times already."

"You mean he's got girl hormones? He's a *chica*?" the guitarist says, motioning toward me.

Sometimes our patients don't tell the whole story, so it's up to us to listen carefully. Nate looks at me, checks to see if anyone else is watching, and then makes a round ball in the air in front of his stomach. We'd read about intersex individuals, but I'd never met one.

"We need to do more tests to figure out why this is happening," Dr. Mehta says.

"Fuck fuck fuck," the young man says. He pinches the skin on his belly, distorting a red dragon, and feels around as if he might find a uterus under there.

"But he has a dick," the guitarist says. "I mean, it's not much, but I've seen it at the gym."

Sometimes our bodies betray us. Something more primal takes over, and the need to reproduce becomes paramount, whether we're prepared for that responsibility or not. I bite the inside of my cheek to keep from getting emotional.

I make an excuse to check on my first patient, the lady in restraints, even though she's not a surgical case. Even in the dim light, I can see that her bed is empty. Clean white sheets, with neatly tucked hospital corners, hide any evidence of her existence. I've managed to lose both of my patients and no one's concerned. I remember the mantra of emergency medicine: treat 'em and street 'em.

In the hallway, my former interpreter mops the floor.

"Where?" I ask, and point to the bed.

"They take her away" is all she says.

Getting here has been an uphill battle. I naively thought, once I was in medical school, I'd work hard and become a good doctor. Not easy, but the path was straightforward. As an undergrad, I spent years in the library. While my business or English major friends took shots of Southern Comfort in their dorm rooms, I'd be slaving over my organic chemistry homework. Orgo was my nemesis, but I won the battle eventually. And when I wasn't studying, I was volunteering at the crisis center, playing in the university orchestra, or campaigning for leadership roles in the premed club, the honors society, or student government. All for my med school applications.

As premeds, we were always in competition, fighting to be part of the scant 15 percent of every science class who got As. To my surprise, medical school hasn't been much different. Everyone wants high honors so they get into a top residency program—the only way to really distinguish yourself is to make everyone else look bad. If you get a good residency, you'll have a shot at the best jobs and fellowships.

Needless to say, I haven't had any meaningful personal relationships. I dated a couple of guys but never had the time or emotional energy to commit. What's the point if he's just competition for your ultimate goal?

I return to observe the ultrasound. Dr. Mehta spreads the jelly all over the young man's abdomen and presses the wand over the red dragon of his belly. There's nothing identifiable on the screen, just grainy white pulses. Dr. Mehta stops. He clicks on the screen. In the chaos, it seems he's forgotten to teach us anything.

"There," he mumbles. "Good fetal heartbeat."

We all see the curled fetus, its disproportionately large head and tiny, amphibious limbs. It's squirming.

"That's disgusting," the young man says. "Get it out of me."

"Termination?" Nate says. "Let's get my resident in here and talk about options. This is a very unusual case."

"I want an abortion. Or whatever you want to call it. Where do I sign?"

"We'll have to do a surgical procedure. My guess is you're

about twelve weeks along," says Dr. Mehta. "Would you like us to call anyone for you?"

"No. This is insane. I'll cut it out myself if I have to."

Krista swoops in, checks his IV fluids, and waits for further orders. I try to remember embryology in case Mehta tests me. Or maybe he'll pimp me on the common forms of inter-sexuality.

"Everything else looks quite healthy and your body seems to be tolerating it. Beautiful uterus," Dr. Mehta says. "There may be other options."

"I'm sure about this," the young man says, exhaling. He digs his fingers into his abdomen. "Get out of my body, you little alien."

"Get the OB resident on call. And," Dr. Mehta says, turning toward me, "page your friends for a surgical consult."

Nate points to the rust-brown stain on my lapel. I've been walking around with Mr. Harper's blood on my pretend doctor's coat.

I sit on the locker room bench, in the dark, hoping to be tele-ported to pediatrics. Kids are loud but relatively simple. If you surprise them before the pain, it hurts a lot less. Outside, the black sky is pouring rain. We're still on generator power. I'm beginning to think my first patient was right and the world is coming to an end, or at least turning upside down. Even though I'm not a superstitious person, the curious pattern—a babbling older woman, a man physically abused by his con-trite wife, and a pregnant young guy—makes me uneasy. I'd been expecting multiple traumas, from car accidents in the blinding rain, maybe even a lightning-strike injury. The locker room door opens, revealing a sliver of light and Nate's eager expression.

"Can you believe this shit?" he says. "My chief resident and general surge were fighting over who gets to do it. Problem is we're swamped and had to give it to them. But they're letting me scrub in on pregnant dude."

"Good."

"What's your problem?"

"I'm tired." It's difficult to believe that he's not getting the hint.

"Too tired for this?" he asks, lifting my scrub top and tracing a Z with his tongue, just below my belly button.

"Jesus, how can you be horny right now?" My eyes have readjusted to the dark. Nate puts his glasses back on. He looks hurt, as if I've offended him.

"I thought it would be a nice distraction," he says.

At this point, sex is the furthest thing from what I want. I feel the sting of hunger in my stomach and realize I haven't eaten in hours. Since I tend to crave sugar, I hope that I still have one of those honey sticks filched from the coffee bar. I seem to remember reading, in terms of hierarchy of needs, that men go for sex first, then food. With women it's the opposite: sustenance is paramount, then comes mating.

"Is it true about all the stillbirths?" I ask Nate.

"Yeah. Three in a row. The last one was really fucked up. Congenital malformations. And mom didn't have prenatal care."

"That's sad."

"What's sad is our tattoo kid. How many hermaphrodites are even fertile? Can you imagine this pregnancy going to term? He'd be famous in the literature."

"And you'd get your pick of residencies."

"He won't tell us anything. Not even why. I mean, how hard is it to have a baby? Crack moms do it."

"Maybe he's not ready. Maybe he wouldn't be a good parent." I close my eyes. Nate makes the situation sound so simple and neat. But it's a sticky web of factors, everything connected like the double helix of DNA.

"I get it," Nate says. "I don't have a uterus so I could never understand."

"Have you ever gotten a girl pregnant?" I ask. This is hitting too close to home for me.

Last year, Jessica, a classmate and friend of mine, was in a relationship with one of the surgical residents. When she got pregnant, she agonized over what to do. I drove her to Planned Parenthood—her regular gyn didn't perform abortions—and I waited for her under the wall of STD pamphlets: *Nervous about herpes?* But Jessica decided not to go through with it. Her surgeon-in-training boyfriend wasn't thrilled, but he played the gallant father by marrying her at city hall. Jessica planned to take six weeks of medical leave after she gave birth, then continue her third-year clinical rotations with the rest of our class. She had to call me several times, sobbing and sleep deprived, because her daycare wouldn't take an infant with rotavirus, and if I didn't have a shift that day could I please, please take him? I helped when I could, but she had to take a leave of absence after failing to show for her last two rotations. When (or if) she finishes, she'll be funneled into one of the softer residencies, like peds or OB.

Just three months ago, I got pregnant after a fling with a law student. The decision should've been easy. I'd sacrificed far too much pursuing medicine—why wouldn't I sacrifice a family too? I blamed myself, because I'd taken a dose of my birth control almost twelve hours late—after a long shift in neurology, I collapsed on my bed before remembering to take my pill.

My tattooed patient couldn't have a baby, just as I couldn't be a single mother in medical school.

"I always use protection," Nate says, interrupting my

thoughts. "And I know how human reproduction works. What're you saying?"

"Calm down. Just because we had sex a few times on your futon doesn't mean you got me pregnant." Nate's giving me a headache.

"Then make me understand. Use your special woman's empathy to know how I'm feeling, and then enlighten me."

"Fuck off."

"That's not very empathetic. I'm going to prep for surgery," Nate says, leaving me alone in the dark.

I get a page from surgery and a cocky intern orders me to get informed consent from our pregnant man. The pre-op area is strangely quiet, except for the occasional rumble of thunder. The muted light casts boxy shadows on the walls.

"How're you doing?" I approach his gurney.

"Fine. Whatever."

"Nice ink," I say, trying to forge some kind of bond. But already I feel stupid because I heard this phrase on TV and have never actually used it.

"Thanks. I'm supposed to get more tomorrow, but I guess that's not an option."

"Where do you get yours done?"

"Red's Tattoo on Liberty. Ask for Karma if you want something with fine detail. Diego's good too."

"I was thinking about getting a caduceus," I say, "you know that medical symbol with a serpent? Right on my chest, so I can open up my lab coat and be like Superman."

He laughs and it sounds genuine. Another minor victory.

"We should probably talk about surgery and risks," I continue. "We need to go over this consent form."

"Where do I sign?"

"You could have an allergic reaction to the anesthesia," I say, "or acquire an infection."

He interrupts. "I know there are risks inherent to surgery. I also know that I can refuse information."

He's correct, but it's still hard to fathom that a person would refuse. "You don't want to be informed?" I ask.

"Nope, just get it over with."

"Sign here." His signature sprawls across the black line, the letters big and angular.

"I didn't ask for this, you know," he says.

"I do know. I'm sorry you've had to make a difficult decision."

"Wasn't difficult," he replies. "Easy peasy."

The anesthesiologist appears, already masked, ready to escort the young man to dream world.

I find sanctuary in a supply closet. The smell of fresh linens comforts me. I can't see anything, which is fine, because I'm trying to pull myself together. I channel the image of a smart, confident physician. Dr. Zoe Savage. I made a choice, and it was medicine. If I'm going to be a doctor, I'd better start acting like one.

I take the stairs, two at a time, to reach the scrub room. Although it's generally bad form for a student to join midprocedure, one of the nurses says they're expecting me. I never look forward to scrubbing my hands raw, but this time I find the motions hypnotic. Twenty times on each side of a finger, then ten, then three. Back and forth, quick strokes, a strange rhythm. My skin tingles with anticipation.

I hold my arms above my waist to avoid contamination and push my hip into the door of OR 1. They're well into the surgery. The operating theater is bright like an interrogation room—I feel strong, rejuvenated by the intense light. A scrub nurse greets me with a sterile gown and I thrust my arms into it. The gown envelops my body, giving me a newfound sense of authority.

"Glove size?" he says.

"Six."

He holds the right glove and I push my rigid fingers into the latex. The glove goes on with a satisfying snap. Then the left, the finishing touch.

Everyone is swathed in blue—scrubs, surgical caps, sterile drapes. I don't know the attending or the surgical resident, but they're both women, a rarity in the macho field of surgery. I can only see their eyes, both of them focused on the task like birds of prey. Nate holds a retractor, pulling open the abdomen, revealing healthy pink viscera. He explains, through his mask, that they're trying to separate the placenta from the uterus.

Surgery is messy and primal. I'd never cared for it before, but I find myself inexplicably drawn to the gore. After all, I'd plunged a needle into a man's bleeding scalp and sewn it back together. Here in the OR, the smell of burning flesh lingers. One surgeon cauterizes while the other suctions the smoke from the smoldering flesh.

"Name the maternal tissue of the basal plate, geniuses," says the cauterizing surgeon.

"Decidua basalis," I answer, before Nate has a chance to even process the question.

"Notable because?"

"In extrauterine pregnancy, a decidual cast may form." I beat him again. The future Dr. Savage: 2. Nate: 0.

Before this procedure, I'd thought of surgery as violent, invading the sacred inner spaces of the human body. But we're the real healers, taking over when the body can't fix itself. Malignancy? Cut it out, using time-honored techniques. We're helping this young man get his life back.

"I'm not sure I can do this," Nate whispers.

"What is this," the cauterizing surgeon says, "time for girl talk, Chatty Cathy?"

"The more you speak, the more moisture builds up in your mask. Less sterile," says the other surgeon. "Silence is golden."

"Do something useful, Nick. Make sure the tissue is accounted for," says the cauterizing surgeon, pointing to a stainless steel dish full of blood.

Nate passes the retractor to me and retrieves the dish. Now I'm the only thing keeping the muscles and fat and guts in place. The thrill (and power) courses through me.

Nate swirls the blood around in the dish, and there it is, a translucent little humanoid that could fit in the palm of my hand. It's hideous. Somehow, I expect it to move. It's mostly head, an encephalus developing under the clear membranes, but there are distinct riblets and a curved spine. Tiny feet and a webbed alien hand. The other miniature arm floats nearby, an accidental amputation from the surgery. It's both wondrous and repulsive.

Sweat beads on Nate's forehead. He turns and vomits in his mask.

"Out," a surgeon yells, "get him the fuck out!"

I can't help but laugh at his vagal response. I never expected him to be soft, especially in a fascinating case like this.

"Surgery's not for everyone," I say, with a hint of contempt. "The tissue's all here, eight centimeters. Looks approximately twelve weeks."

"Good," the cauterizing surgeon says. "I hear you have a badass running suture, Savage. You doing a surgical elective?"

"I don't know."

"Consider it."

They let me suction now. I use the tool to vacuum smoke from the air, the burning particles of carbon that were once this young man's flesh. Circle of life and all that. Suddenly I picture Nate taking off his surgical scrubs. All I can think about is his toned chest and the way he likes it when I kiss his nipples.

I find him in the dark locker room. I reach for my penlight, which I'd normally use to check a patient's pupils, and click it on. Nate squints. His hair is wet and he smells of Ivory soap.

"Did you have any hot water?" I ask.

"Electricity's back on."

In all the excitement, I didn't notice. "Why'd you turn the lights off then?"

He shrugs.

"You okay?"

"Yeah," he says. He's putting Visine in his eyes, liquid teardrops, as though weeping in reverse. Then he looks at me, bleary-eyed.

"You're sitting in the dark, crying, but you're okay?"

I can't imagine he's broken up about the patient, so maybe he's upset about being kicked out of the OR. I didn't know he was such a pussy.

"You sure you're okay?"

"I'm fine."

"You don't look fine," I say, "but I know what will cheer you up." I peel off his new scrub top, then slip my hands under his drawstring waistband. The chemical tang of bleach makes me take off his pants too. I want to smell his skin.

"I'm not really in the mood."

I straddle him anyway. He'll change his mind. I reach for the condom in the left zipper pocket of his backpack.

"Hush," I say. "You know, it's not the end of the world."

Incendiary Girls

I'M NOT OFTEN wrong—after all, I've been doing this thankless job for thousands of years. Humans are nothing if not predictable, especially as they near their end. There's no meeting of the maker, as some stubborn humans believe, but they do get to meet me, or one of my kind. Suffice it to say that humans have a difficult time with the transition, being social animals and all—consider me an escort. It's probably easiest to think of me as an angel of death, since you may be familiar with that concept. Given my vast experience, my assessments are generally swift and accurate. But of the times I've been incorrect, a few cases stand out.

The other "angels" and I don't have much to entertain ourselves, so I admit, we bet on the exact times and ways in which we'll meet certain humans. For one such girl, I predicted I'd take her from typhus, age twelve, several weeks before the grape harvest. My friend and colleague said, oh, no, a transportation accident of some kind, sixteen years old. My other friend predicted violence, by a man scorned, and age twelve sounded right.

Sure, twelve is a bit young, even by early twentieth-century standards, but men have been impatient ever since the start of the species. In any case, she seemed destined to meet one of us sooner rather than later. She had that look about her, darting eyes that took in everything, then told her to escape at whatever cost, like a horse that would rather break her forelegs than submit to the harness.

I saw those wild eyes when I first came for her, as a newborn hardly expelled from her mother's womb. Cord wrapped around the baby's neck, the midwife's apprentice silently practicing her condolences, not yet comfortable delivering bad news. Just as it was my cue—I'd been assigned the Near East that night—the gray skin bloomed pink, and her eyes cracked open, pale blue as the base of a candle's flame.

Now, before you think I'm a monster, I have to say that I abhor taking children. We all do. But sometimes the corporeal flesh is just too weak. Only when we know there's no chance—oxygen has left the lungs, the last neurons of consciousness have fired—do we swoop in to do our job. We'd much rather take the older folks, the humans who've lived long enough to have regrets. Not the children, who have yet to regret anything. The only "blessing," in human religious parlance, is that most kids are too young to be scared of us.

I have no doubt that this early mishap, of the cord wrapped around her neck, influenced our wagers. The babies who survive a difficult birth sometimes reveal their strength and have a long life, but most use up all their vital energy in the birth trauma and die young. We all agreed the girl, later christened Vartouhi, or "rose maiden," would meet one of us before adulthood. Little did we know that she and her people would be subjected to the first genocide of the twentieth century.

Of course, we'd seen systematic massacres before, sometimes cross-species but mostly intraspecies. What do you think happened to the Wurlenans or the Burba? Never heard of them? My point exactly. Humans are unique like that. The most famous, or should I say infamous, was perpetrated by German leaders against the Jews, starting in 1941. Modern technology—poison gas, cheap bullets, even the efficient railways—made those mass killings possible. And we had no time to rest in those years. Work, work, work. When we did have any downtime, we tried to predict what creative new methods of torture and murder the Nazis would come up with. Placing those bets, we really, truly, wanted to be wrong, because no living beings should have to undergo such treatment. But sometimes we were correct. God, those sick, twisted fucks.

They weren't the first, obviously, and probably wouldn't be the last group of humans to exterminate another group. We do try to have a sense of humor about this—don't they know they all descend from the same ancestors? That they're all the same people? The smartest species to ever inhabit Earth is also the dumbest, which would be hilarious if humans didn't act on their stupidity.

So yes, Vartouhi and her people became targets. To be fair, if you're looking at ratios, her people were almost completely annihilated—more than three-quarters of the entire population. Those Germans, who thought so highly of their efficiency, managed to kill less than half of the world's Jews. Seventy-five percent of Vartouhi's people? Gone forever.

And without modern technologies. This was 1915, you see. Want to destroy the majority of a population? March them for weeks, preferably in the desert, and wait. They starve, or more likely, wilt and dehydrate like dried flowers. Finally, when every cell in their bodies has given up, we come in. Even *we* were impressed, in a professional capacity. The world had seen nothing quite like it. Later, Hitler would ask his minions if they remembered Vartouhi's people, just days before he invaded Poland. Of course they didn't remember. That was the point. I believe you humans call it a rhetorical question. No one remembers!

That's not exactly true. I remember being so busy that all bets were off. Ridiculous, not a moment for me to stop and think, just death, death, death. Nonstop work. Dying, denial, not so nice to meet you.

Still, before all this, I kept a close eye on Vartouhi. Just twelve years old and nearing her expiration date. She was on the verge of beauty—features a bit exaggerated on her face, eyes cartoonish, limbs still long and thin enough to be called gangly—just a few steps from the precipice of womanhood. Among the dusky girls, she was striking, with her sienna hair and blue eyes. Her mother foresaw this precipice, along with the dangers. But Vartouhi, who had yet to bleed the color of her namesake each month, wanted to grow up as soon as possible. She was accustomed to caring for her younger siblings and didn't see the point of attending the missionary school every day if she was going to raise a family of her own soon.

When the gendarmes appeared at their door one evening and took her father away, along with most every man in the village, her mother told the children a story. While little Elmas cried and Masrope tossed ants into the fireplace and Vartouhi washed the supper dishes, their mother explained that their father was given a new job in the government. He was destined for greatness. In fact, they were all headed for a beautiful new home, but Father was going first to ready the estate for them. Vartouhi listened from the wash sink, both intrigued by her mother's tale and irritated that she was expected to believe it.

As her mother nursed the youngest, baby Hrepsama, she

continued: "We will go on a great adventure and meet him. But first they'll test our strength to make sure we're fit for our new home, where we'll be treated like royalty. Your grandparents, aunts and uncles, your cousins too. Mezes and huge feasts every night."

"Will there be *paklava*?" Elmas asked, pausing between sobs, "and *kanafeh*?"

"Of course."

Satisfied by this answer, Elmas exhaled, blowing a snot bubble from her nose. Masrope wanted to know if he would have his own pony. No, not a pony—a horse.

"Yes," their mother replied. "A full-blooded Arabian. Any color you like. But remember, on our journey, we must survive with very little to eat or drink, to test if we're worthy of the great feasts. We can help our friends, but to pass our test we have to stay strong for each other. Father will be waiting for us."

"So when do we leave?" Vartouhi asked.

Ah, teenage girls. Any human culture, any period in history, always the same. While technically only twelve, in some ways, Vartouhi was mature for her age.

That night, she had to chew her pillow to keep Elmas from hearing her cry. Vartouhi feared her father was dead, or worse—tortured for the sick pleasure of the gendarmes. She prayed his death was quick and merciful. I can tell you that it was neither, but her father's last thoughts were of his wife suckling little Vartouhi, his firstborn and favorite, which he'd tried to hide from the other children. His last sight was of the dusty left boot of a gendarme.

Vartouhi knew none of her father's end. But what happened the next day, she would always remember. Sent by her mother to buy more rice for pilaf, with her sister Elmas tagging along because it was easier to appease her than fight her, they walked past the village square. In the center stood Araxi, the most beautiful girl of the five surrounding towns, flanked by gendarmes.

Vartouhi had always looked up to Araxi, seventeen yet the most powerful woman Vartouhi had ever known, the fodder for boys' dreams and many of the men's fantasies too. Weeks before, Vartouhi had rubbed kohl on her red-brown eyelashes to make them look lush and black just like Araxi's. The effect for Vartouhi, alas, was more clownish than seductive, and Vartouhi's mother punished her by forcing Vartouhi to color her entire face with kohl, even her teeth. Her mother had never enforced a punishment so harsh, and Vartouhi tasted charcoal for days. Vartouhi wanted more than ever to be desired by men and to have a pair of strong arms to hold her when life was unfair.

Now, in the middle of the gendarmes, stood Araxi. As they taunted her, those normally alluring eyes, fringed with dark lashes, refused to look up.

"Dance, whore, dance!" said the gendarme with the most brass on his epaulets. Two others spit on her, and when she raised her hand to wipe the saliva from her face, he grabbed her wrist and twisted until she made the cry of a desert hawk.

"You refuse?" said their leader. "Well, this will make you dance."

Elmas grabbed at Vartouhi's skirt. "What are they doing to her?"

"Shh," Vartouhi whispered, pulling her scarf over her hair. "They're testing her. She might be a princess."

One of the gendarmes produced a can of kerosene and poured the liquid all over Araxi, who fell to the ground in a heap, palms upward, to avoid being drenched. As Vartouhi watched, she wanted to believe her mother's stories, but the reality of what was happening not twenty feet away plucked her from childhood and planted her firmly into the adult realm.

As the gendarme held a match to the village beauty's long, dark hair, Vartouhi spun her little sister around, so the child's eyes were covered by Vartouhi's skirt. But Vartouhi took in the entire horrifying scene. Because I knew it would be at least ninety excruciating seconds before Araxi perished, I went to take an old man a town over, whose heart had beat its last. He wasn't much trouble, of course.

I knew how this immolation would play out. Vartouhi thought the fire would cause death—when the skin had melted off—but she, like so many, was mistaken. How long can you hold your breath? A minute, maybe two? That's how long it takes. Suffocation, that's what brings me near. I don't know how to describe it well in English, because there is no other human sensation like it. When the lungs scream for lack of air, the brain recognizes me: certain death.

In poor Araxi's case, she had to contend with the lack of oxygen, plus the searing flame, cooking her like a spring lamb. Only the spring lamb, as it were, had met me long before and felt none of the painful flame. I don't mean to confuse you. This is what Vartouhi saw first: the blaze orange flame devouring the beauty's dark hair in a bright halo, with the smell of singed locks lingering—Vartouhi's only association with the scent being when she passed the blacksmith's and he was nailing the hot iron to a gelding's hoof. Burned keratin is the same among species.

The initial few seconds weren't painful for Araxi, as the blue lip of the flame rolled from Araxi's forehead in a gentle wave down to her feet. But the enraged red and blaze orange, hungry for oxygen, soon followed in its wake, dancing where Araxi had refused.

Vartouhi watched as the beauty's skin bubbled. This is when the dying girl, with so little oxygen to spare, began to scream. Her pristine skin, coveted by all the boys in a twenty-mile radius as they touched it in their dreams, sloughed off in sheets. Starting with the skin of her neck and right cheek, her shoulders, the fat underneath glistening. Oily black smoke filled the air.

"Is she a princess?" Elmas asked, and on that cue, Vartouhi marched them toward the house. She had a little sister to think of and couldn't afford to be frozen in her own shock. Still, from that point on, Vartouhi vowed to keep her hair pulled back, lest it catch fire. The way her locks shined deep red in the sun, Vartouhi reasoned, was one step closer to the flame.

As the sisters walked back to the house, Vartouhi cupped El-mas's ears between her palms, ensuring that the child couldn't look back.

"Araxi is so good at the test," Vartouhi said, "that maybe she is a queen."

The screams were horrible, but even worse was when they stopped. My cue, obviously, as the escort.

"We know a queen?" Elmas asked. "Queen Araxi and we knew her before she was royalty."

"Yes," Vartouhi replied, determined to continue the ruse. "A queen."

You humans and your precious stories. I suppose I'm not helping, telling one of my own, and I shouldn't criticize, given that narrative is how you make meaning of your lives. Forming a pattern out of chaos, it seems. I don't blame you.

Speaking of chaos, three days later, the family was summoned for their great adventure. The gendarmes allowed them to bring nothing more than the clothes they wore and a single knapsack, in which Vartouhi's mother packed bread, walnuts, and dried apricots, along with all their money and a sheep's bladder of water. Vartouhi carried baby Hrepsama, who gummed the bodice of Vartouhi's wool dress.

"Here we go!" her mother exclaimed, holding the hands of Elmas and Masrope. At that point, Vartouhi questioned everything her mother had ever said. Vartouhi wondered what was truth and what was fiction—what had been sanitized for her consumption. Yet she'd never seen evil quite like this. Not in the form of police who set girls on fire, the very people who were supposed to protect her. Despite her misgivings, Vartouhi wouldn't spoil the fantasy for her siblings.

Along with the other villagers, they walked among the fertile fields and orchards, which eventually gave way to barren hills. When Masrope asked how long the journey would last, their mother replied, "I don't know," the first true words she'd spoken since Vartouhi had questioned her veracity.

The girl's arms and shoulders ached from carrying her baby sister, who'd only fussed when they'd left the village. Hrepsama mostly dozed on Vartouhi's chest, content and drooling. Their mother eventually tied the baby to Vartouhi's back with the blanket, which temporarily alleviated the strain for Vartouhi.

I had my work cut out for me that first day, taking elderly folks and a few children. A young mother too, who set down her toddler for a moment to give her six-year-old a drink of water. A bored gendarme decided her pause was tantamount to treason. At least the bullet was quick and my responsibility was clear. For the infant, less so, as he cried and clutched his dead mother's breast. An auntie shooed along the six-year-old, but those who passed the infant marched on in shock and denial, and the few who thought to pick him up reasoned that they had to save their own. This was not a world where anyone knew the rules or expectations of behavior, only that they had to put one aching foot in front of the other and ignore the arid heat that wrung the moisture from their veins, leaving their mouths tasting of raw cotton.

While their mother attempted to ration the bladder of water, by midafternoon, it was only one-third full. Vartouhi and Masrope walked behind their mother, now carrying Elmas, Masrope insisting he was too old to hold hands with anyone. For his sake, Vartouhi hoped he believed they were headed for a grand new home. She could smell that the baby was soiled and she wanted to think about something else, anything else, even her mother's lies.

"What color mare will you choose?" she asked him. The never-ending horizon spread before them, interrupted by craggy hills. Every time she saw the brush as flame rather than foliage, fear clawed her chest. She imagined the dry grass sparking a fire, licking their skirts and setting the entire caravan alight.

"Black," Masrope finally replied. "Like my hair. Like Father's beard."

"With a white blaze?" As she said the word "blaze," she conjured pale fire in her mind. Then she reached up to check her hair, braided into a plait then coiled into a tight bun, safely at the back of her neck. Her shoulder locked into a cramp before she could stretch it. Thankfully, none of this disrupted Hrepsama's slumber.

"No, I changed my mind," Masrope said. "Gray. Dapple gray."

"How old?"

"Two or three, just broken for the saddle."

Vartouhi touched her careful chignon again, which would become a compulsion. To her relief, it wasn't any warmer than Masrope's hair.

"I have to pee," he said.

"Hold it as long as you can."

"I *have*," he said, as if Vartouhi were an idiot.

"Then you'll have to pee down your leg."

Masrope scoffed. "That's disgusting."

"It's part of the test. How much do you want that mare?"

"I want my horse," he said, then whispered, "I don't want to end up like Mrs. Hagopian. They failed, right?" He was referring to the young mother and infant who'd paused.

"Oh," said Vartouhi. "Yes, they failed the test."

As they walked, Masrope kept looking down at his pants, as if willing the wet spot on his crotch to stop expanding. When the tears of shame welled in his eyes, it was all Vartouhi could do to keep them at bay herself. Before her father was taken away, he told her never to hate. Remember, but never hate. It was only then that Vartouhi suspected her rising fears were valid and that most of them would be realized.

As the sun began its descent, bringing a welcome chill to the air, Vartouhi chewed on a dried apricot. She'd sucked all the moisture from it and failing in her determination to make it last an hour, started to chew the sweet fruit but it stuck to her molars. Periodically, her mother and Elmas would look back. During one of those checks, her mother mimed wiping her nose. When Vartouhi did the same, the back of her hand came away crimson, blood dripping from her nostril. She had only her skirt to dam the flow, and she lifted the hem to her nose to make the bleeding stop, careful to balance the load on her back as she did so.

"It's okay," Masrope said, wrapping a thin arm around her. "You got an easy test today."

"I did," she said, and for the second time that day, Vartouhi bit into the flesh of her index finger to keep from crying. She was aware that her shins and knees were exposed, but what did it matter? Over the course of the next hour, checking for fresh blood that bloomed bright red against the burgundy stain, Vartouhi began to panic, but the bleeding ceased. She didn't understand why it had to come from her nose and not where it was supposed to come from, if she were a woman. Not only must she undergo this journey, but as a child, no less. Carrying another on her back.

When the convoy stopped for the night — after all, the gendarmes' horses had been walking all day — Vartouhi and her family waited for the others to sit before falling to the ground. Night, already so dark that Vartouhi couldn't see the dust in which she sat. Elmas and Masrope sank into sleep quickly. Before her mother nursed Hrepsama, she pressed four coins into Vartouhi's palm.

"Keep these in the only secret place you have, yes?"

Vartouhi agreed several seconds before she realized what her mother meant. Of course she would, although it made for an awkward few minutes as Vartouhi lay on her side, shoving the coins into herself, terrified they'd fall out when she stood up. She steeled herself for the possible consequences by the time her breathing slowed and eyelids fell heavy to her cheekbones.

I was here and there, but always watching Vartouhi for signs of the end. Or illness, as I'd wagered with my friends. She seemed as healthy as possible, given the situation. But we all know how quickly these things can change.

The next days passed as the first for Vartouhi's family, with aching feet, blistering skin, parched throats, and the constant roil of their stomachs. When they ambled through the villages, sometimes they'd be robbed — this was how the family lost all their money, except for the coins hidden by Vartouhi. Sometimes they'd be spat upon. Desperate for water, Vartouhi once wiped the spit from her cheek and swallowed it. She even considered stealing the saliva from baby Hrepsama, before guilt and shame prevented her. Vartouhi tried sucking the blood from her skirt, then the urine, before she started seeing her mother and Elmas in flames. Her own hair felt so hot that she steeled herself for the moment she'd catch fire.

One evening, her mother suddenly turned into a horned ewe. Her brother, a small brown bear, and her sisters two little hedgehogs. Some village men stripped her mother, the ewe, of all her wool. Vartouhi could only watch from where she lay on the ground. The larger hedgehog tried to keep her company, curling into Vartouhi's armpit, but the little animal was so hot on her skin that Vartouhi had to shoo it away.

Everything was searing, even the ground, usually so cool and comforting. Her raging fever gave me a smug satisfaction—it wouldn't be long before I'd won the bet. But then a marauding thug approached her, intent on getting his due.

Vartouhi screamed, "I have no wool! See, my skin is shorn. No wool for you to take!"

In the light of the full moon, he saw the dried blood on her skirt, then muttered something and kicked her in the ribs with a force that knocked the air from her lungs. I cursed my friend, who'd predicted violence by a scorned man.

After a moment of panic, Vartouhi was able to inhale oxygen again. Her scalp still burned. It was clear that the kick had caused only a few bruises and that her fever was much more threatening. Now the ewe stood over her and spoke:

"Oh, my sweet rose. My firstborn. This is just a touch of sickness. You've known worse, remember? The fever will break soon. Be strong."

In the early hours of the morning, Vartouhi recognized me. She refused, no no no *no*, figuratively kicking and screaming. Her body weak and her mind fuzzy, I thought I was victorious. Remember, I'd predicted typhus, age twelve? I was already gloating to my fellow angels in my head—the beating was secondary. We had nothing to wager but our pride and dignity, so as you can imagine, the stakes were high. Something in that cloudy mind and fragile body rallied, a survival instinct, her fear and hatred of me strong enough to overcome her corporeal reality. Her only thorn, pitiful armor, a lone barb that managed to catch my sleeve and unravel the fabric of her fate.

She awoke to the milky blue light of dawn. Vartouhi eyed the fading stars with suspicion, unsure if they were of her world or another. Her little sister Elmas, no longer a hedgehog, snored softly at her hip. Vartouhi wanted to hug the girl until their ribs cracked. She felt the particular joy that only comes after seeing me, a jolt that coursed through her like an electric shock. A breeze slapped Vartouhi's face, and her eyelashes caught the rising sun, making a gauzy rainbow like an exotic butterfly's wings in her peripheral vision. Even the dried apricot she allowed herself tasted like manna, despite Elmas's insistence that the desiccated fruit looked like an ear.

"You had a hard test yesterday. So did Mama. But you passed," Elmas said.

"Yes," said Vartouhi, only now remembering what had been done to her mother. "Yes, we did well. And so will you. There's more to come."

They'd both survived and the family remained intact. For this, Vartouhi was so grateful that she wanted to embrace the bearded gendarme ten feet ahead of them, but thought better of the idea.

While Vartouhi enjoyed the day, I became increasingly busy. I had to take a baby that'd been growing in his mother's belly for eight months, knowing I'd be back soon for his mother. Then an old woman who'd fought me for several years finally succumbed, undignified, to heatstroke.

I had my eye on Hrepsama, who rarely made a sound now. Their mother's milk had long dried up. Vartouhi rubbed the infant's lips and pressed a bit of chewed apricot to them, but her sister refused to eat. Vartouhi wished she could give her crushed mulberries, the baby's favorite, but she hadn't seen a ripe mulberry tree for weeks.

That afternoon, the gendarmes paused for a few minutes so they could relieve themselves (they'd eaten undercooked lamb in the last village). Vartouhi's mother tried, for a final time, to nurse Hrepsama. The baby's skin, usually rosy olive, looked ashen. Vartouhi resolved to offer herself for food or money at the next village, anything to sustain her family and save her sister. They'd need the gold coins for a tent once they arrived at the refugee camp, or wherever they ended up, so Vartouhi would save those.

Hrepsama's end was imminent, I knew with certainty. She came with me willingly, as most babies do, her body unable to produce even a soft gurgle or make the effort to uncurl her fingers. I surrounded her from all sides, as if I were a comforting womb. I hate taking children, as I said before, and the act feels particularly heinous when the death is caused by man, as was the case here.

As the convoy began to move again, Vartouhi could bear the weight no longer.

"She's too heavy," she whispered to her mother.

"*Doostr,*" said her mother, who'd felt the same burden, "place the little one under the shade of this bush."

"No, I'll carry her," Vartouhi volunteered. "Tie her to my back. Please, Mama."

Meanwhile, two gendarmes pressed their bayonets toward them, ordering them to move. The infant's body, sliding from Vartouhi's arms, would be crushed under their feet.

"Leave her," her mother whispered, out of earshot of Vartouhi's siblings. "Don't worry. You're only the sister. You will

forget." She helped Vartouhi set the dead baby under an arbutus bush, long stripped of its berries.

Vartouhi felt the point of a bayonet at her back as her
mother grabbed Elmas's hand and pulled the girl forward.
"This is too much for Hrepsama. We'll come back for her tonight."

"Too much for her," Elmas echoed, looking over her shoulder at Vartouhi.

"Please," Vartouhi said, but she fell in line with her mother
and Elmas. The girl was obviously in denial that I'd taken her
darling baby sister. A fairly common reaction, to be honest.
Not to mention the fact that Vartouhi had just gotten a second
chance at life herself. She still had hope.

Beside her, Masrope extended a hand, which Vartouhi accepted. She vowed to come back for Hrepsama that night,
memorizing the shape of the arbutus bush, its oblong leaves
all pointing toward the sun. The bush grew just off the place
where the road curled like a poked silkworm. Vartouhi com-
mitted every detail to memory.

When the gendarmes decided their horses had had enough
for the day, Vartouhi retraced her steps back to Hrepsama
in her mind as the rest of her family prepared for sleep. She
closed her eyes to visualize the journey better, and when she
opened them, her mother and another older lady stood before her.

"Sit. Hold out your hands," her mother commanded.

Vartouhi obeyed. Her mother knelt and untied the apron
that, in their haste, she'd forgotten to take off when they left
home. She then wove it around Vartouhi's wrists. Thinking it
was some kind of game for the kids, Vartouhi laughed. But
the village lady started to bind Vartouhi's ankles together with
a man's wool sash. Far from a joke, Vartouhi realized that they

were preventing her from going back, and she'd never see her baby sister again. Poor Hrepsama, all alone in the chilly night air, the distant stars giving no warmth or comfort. Vartouhi shuddered to think the infant wouldn't get a proper burial. Or worse, that her corpse might be burned to ash.

Vartouhi, bound and impotent, pulled her body into a fetal position, making herself as small as she felt. The day, which had started with such promise, ended with the numbness of grief. I know grief well, for nearly all humans mourn the loss of their world. But Vartouhi had not yet lost hers—that was still to come.

That next night, the convoy stopped just outside a small enclave. Village thugs—boys, really—robbed the Shoushanians and the Papazians, for they were the only families with any money left. Vartouhi, with those four coins deep inside her, feared what they might do to get the money.

As if sensing that fear, a village woman approached Vartouhi's mother. The woman, hair covered in a scarf, knew a bit of their language, and Vartouhi overheard them speaking:

"Oh, yes, safe. Keep her, I will, then you return."

Her mother, probably reassured that the woman spoke their language, at least in broken phrases, said: "Please take good care of her. She's the rose of my garden. Do you understand? My daughter is very special."

Whatever her mother saw in Vartouhi, I had yet to pinpoint. Yes, I'd grown fond of the girl, but only because she'd defied my expectations and undermined our wager, the cheeky little thing. So the fondness was more for her tenacity than anything else, like the weed you've pulled out by the roots and keeps growing back.

Vartouhi found herself saying good-bye to Elmas and Masrope. She chewed the inside of her cheek to keep from showing any emotion. But the worst of it came when her mother refused to break character, wouldn't drop the charade: "No reason to be sad. We'll meet you at our new estate with Papa."

"Yes," Vartouhi croaked, "see you then."

The village woman, Fatema, pulled Vartouhi by the elbow. As they walked away from the encampment, Fatema took a more direct approach, gripping Vartouhi's earlobe. The woman finally released her grip as she arranged a gray scarf to cover Vartouhi's hair. In fact, Vartouhi had begun to envy the headscarves, because they appeared to protect the wearer from any flame.

"You always wear, yes?" the woman said.

Vartouhi nodded in agreement, but in those minutes she'd agree to anything, for she'd just lost the only family she'd ever known. Without that compass to guide her, she felt the reeling vertigo of uncertainty.

Knowing that Vartouhi wasn't in imminent danger, I had to move on to more pressing matters. I checked on her periodically, learning that Fatema sold her to a family to be their house servant. Since Vartouhi wasn't paid, slave was a more accurate term for her position. Her master, Muhammad, was kind enough and Vartouhi was grateful that he didn't molest her. He had two wives, so the house was divided into two apartments, joined by a central courtyard. The outdoor space contained olive trees and a fountain, and would've been a peaceful respite had the two wives not used the area to bicker over Vartouhi. Each wanted Vartouhi for herself—the first wife tried to pull rank while the second felt superior and in more need of the girl's services because she had a four-year-old son.

Vartouhi learned to prostrate before a different god (not that she believed in one by this point), began to bleed every month, and told herself stories to keep from using the butcher knife to drain the veins in her wrist. I think the idea of meeting me again was the ultimate deterrent. She no longer desired a man's touch, not after the desert raids and seeing the pain it could bring. But maybe she'd enjoy the touch of a prince — maybe her mother had been right all along, that self-delusion was the only appropriate antidote for fear and boredom. This was all just a test to see if Vartouhi was worthy.

The houseboy learned of Vartouhi's pyrophobia, because she always asked him to light the fire and she stayed a respectable distance away. In an effort to impress her, he did so pre-emptively. She appreciated his help, which lightened her burden but didn't bring her happiness.

Her only joy came in the early hours of the morning, when Vartouhi would take the master's mare, Sultana, to gallop in the hills. When she first saw the animal, Vartouhi wept, for the animal was a gray Arabian with a sprinkling of lighter dapples on her back and haunches. Vartouhi had to believe this was more than coincidence, that Masrope's horse preference meant something, that against all odds, her family was alive and well.

In those predawn rides, Vartouhi held the reins only for guidance, because she let the mare take the bit and run. They rarely saw others on these rides — sometimes a fellow servant, and once the baker, but his conspiratorial glance told her that he'd never share the secret.

The exhilaration she felt — the sheer joy from having no one tell her what to do, the wind in her face as she gained speed — all of it was ecstasy. Vartouhi had power for the first time in her young life. She lived for those moments, sailing the indigo sky, daring the sun to show its face. The mare, for her part, would snort and raise her tail toward the heavens, a challenge if there ever was one. On these rides, Sultana might buck a time or two, but only in excitement. By then, Vartouhi was an experienced rider and felt when Sultana was happy, but also the occasional times the horse was afraid.

They were a symbiotic pair, two became one. On the rare times that Vartouhi felt fear, so did Sultana. One early morning, as they rounded a copse of trees, Vartouhi spied a fire in the distance. Without warning, her stomach rose and that familiar fear clawed at her chest. The horse, sensing Vartouhi's apprehension, lunged sideways and upward simultaneously. Before Vartouhi could react, she was falling backward, her head slamming against the ground.

I'd lost track of Vartouhi's age. The year was 1919, which put her at sixteen years old. Transportation accident—of course. I'd also grown fonder of the girl, maybe even affectionate toward her. Even so, I wasn't about to let my friend win this wager. I'd influence the girl however possible.

Young girl, I told her, this is not your time. Rise up. You have the blood of many strong men and women, a lineage of hardy storytellers who depend on your survival. How will they live on if you do not? You entered this world with the cord choking your neck, blue-faced, fists clenched, and I won't permit you to leave it so easily.

She didn't stir. Now, I don't usually give encouragement—not part of the job description—so I had no idea if my communication was effective. Hope was not an emotion I'd experienced, and in fact, one that I actively avoided. Hope is for humans and other animals that are intelligent enough to have foresight but just delusional enough to ignore the warning signs.

I used to believe that humans never really changed. Not so! With the help of science, they've become more efficient at killing each other—A-bombs, H-bombs, drones. To be fair, humans have also gotten much better at saving lives as well. Did I mention that doctors are now the bane of my existence? In simpler times, I knew when someone with pneumonia would take his last breath. Now they have the miracle drugs, beginning with penicillin, the humble mold that started it all. I suppose humans are learning to work with nature rather than against it. Of course, nature has the upper hand, with massive earthquakes, tsunamis, epidemics, and such. All of it overtime work for my kind.

And horses, while domesticated by man, still harbor the destructive power of the natural world. Any equine can kill a grown man with a kick to the chest. Or, in Vartouhi's case, a fall from the mare's back and the force of hitting the ground at just the right angle.

Either my pep talk worked, or Vartouhi had a resilient skull, or a touch of both, because she awoke to the light of dawn and two men standing over her. When one man asked if she was okay in her native tongue (which she hadn't heard in nearly four years), Vartouhi was convinced that she was dead and in heaven.

Instead of answering him, in the off chance that she was still alive, she yelled, "Where is the gray mare?" Still on her back and suddenly feeling the air inflate her lungs, she knew she'd be beaten, or worse, for her transgressions.

"Right here. I have her," said the man. Vartouhi saw the underside of the horse's jaw, and the man's fingers wrapped around the reins, looming in her peripheral vision. She felt a wash of relief — she didn't lose the mare, so Vartouhi's life would be spared. Then she noticed the earnest brown eyes of her Good Samaritan and saw the kind reflection of her father, her grandparents, her entire family.

I was just glad to see the girl was fine and that my friend hadn't won the bet. An ill-fated transportation accident, age sixteen, death averted, at least for now. Then I realized she still had another two months until turning seventeen. And I couldn't protect her, only observe from afar.

Her Good Samaritan, it turned out, had traveled from America back to the land of his birth to find a bride. Like his fellow immigrants, he knew of the atrocities in his homeland and rumors of all the orphaned girls. It only seemed right to share the abundance of America, and his relative wealth, with a girl who'd lost everything. After all, few of his people remained. So when he brought Vartouhi and Sultana back to Muhammad, he offered a fair price for the girl.

Vartouhi had no say in the matter but laughed to herself, because her mother had been right all along—tales were useful if you believed them. Vartouhi decided, then and there, that her prince had arrived. So what if he was a barber who lived in Detroit? She was going to America!

Before she left, the sweet houseboy gave her a little box of matches so she could practice. Vartouhi knew she'd have to face her fears sooner rather than later. What if she had to light candles? What if she had a gas stove in her new home?

During the two-month voyage, I checked on her nearly every day. For the first weeks, Vartouhi was seasick and losing the extra flesh in her cheeks and hips. All the while she actually missed wearing the headscarf, because it added an extra layer of protection from any errant flame. Vartouhi felt naked without it, as if a candle flame might leap from the wick and devour her tendrils in a searing halo.

Then came the epidemic of Spanish flu on the ship. Unlike most contagions, I took the healthiest people first. The more robust one's immune system, the worse the attack. I escorted mostly young men and some women. Vartouhi felt more exhausted than usual, falling asleep on her feet, her head aching, and now convinced she'd never make it to her new home, because the immigration doctors wouldn't allow her into the country. Or worse—they'd send her back.

For his part, her new husband doted on her, rubbing her temples and fetching fresh water. But Vartouhi felt best when she stood on the deck and gazed at the vast expanse of blue. The sheer quantity of water comforted her. How could a flame ever catch her with all this water as protection? She fingered the box of matches in her pocket. In another pocket, she kept the four coins she'd carried all these years. When she threw them into the ocean, she said a prayer for her mother, Masrope, Elmas, and Hrepsama.

I, for one, was still worried about a fateful accident—the ship's boiler exploding, or a collision with another vessel. I watched as Vartouhi grew bolder, once even opening the box and examining a match—the innocuous little head, the pale wooden stick, on the whole a benign, simple item, but capable of such pain and destruction.

One afternoon on the deck, a young woman approached Vartouhi.

"Can I beg a light?" she asked in Vartouhi's adopted tongue, the language of her captors. The woman had dark hair the color of a ripe walnut shell spilling down her back in a loose braid.

"Oh," Vartouhi replied, realizing she hated that language and everyone who spoke it, "don't get too close. I may be sick."

"Don't worry," the woman said, gesticulating with her cigarette, "I've already had the influenza." The wind whipped strands of her hair free from the braid, until most of it was loose. And vulnerable to flame.

Vartouhi knew that spontaneous combustion wasn't likely, but deliberate ignition was a possibility. If someone created a flame—by way of a candle or a match—this woman could become a searing halo of light. Her death could be delicious revenge, for her people had destroyed so many of Vartouhi's people, Vartouhi's family, and Vartouhi's world.

But was Vartouhi capable of sending another human to her death, to the realm over which I preside? Most humans are, in fact, capable of murder when driven to extremes. Or as we've seen in the genocidal twentieth century, people are capable when the right authority holds sway.

Vartouhi cupped the matchbox in her left hand and pushed it open. Pinching a single match between her thumb and forefinger, she examined the little splinter of wood that could start a fire and melt the skin from a girl's face. Or the smirk from this woman's face.

Vartouhi pressed the match to the striking edge and the flame appeared, just inches from the woman's locks. The power, now at Vartouhi's fingertips, the hungry fire so close to the woman's dark hair. Revenge, if she acted at this moment.

Vartouhi's authority was moral, rather than mortal. While she wanted nothing more than to exact revenge for the loss of her family, she knew that seeing more pain wouldn't bring any lasting satisfaction.

With a flick of her wrist, the woman's cigarette met the flame and the cherry glowed red. The wind quickly blew the match out. Vartouhi knew she'd have to make up a new story for herself and, most important, believe it.

"May I?" she asked. The woman handed her the cigarette. Vartouhi, the smoke tickling her throat, decided that every inhalation gave her strength and control over destruction. Every breath of warm smoke gave her control over evil in the world.

The next day, she turned seventeen. I'm not superstitious, obviously, but it felt like a victory. Vartouhi continued to smoke, because it was the only thing that gave her comfort. And it turned out she wasn't sick. When they docked in the United States, the immigration doctor happened to be from the old country, one of their people. Even if she'd had the influenza, he wasn't about to send her back to that hell. He did a more thorough examination than usual and gave his congratulations, for she was expecting.

This was one of the few times that I welcomed a doctor's interference. Against all odds, she was not only pregnant, but she'd live to old age. Vartouhi eventually had four children, each birth quiet and uneventful, as I kept vigil.

She allowed herself one cigarette per week during her pregnancies, having become dependent on the ritual, but mostly because she remained superstitious. Smoking, that controlled burn, gave her power, her own little light in all the darkness.

Vartouhi was even able to light her children's birthday candles without fear. On the Fourth of July, she could watch them play in the yard with sparklers. And because they were safe, they never had to hear stories of long journeys or difficult tests or grand estates. Of course that logic wasn't sound, but what use is logic to a genocide survivor? There is no rhyme or reason for what happened. I've made a narrative and I still can't figure it out.

Her children eventually formed their own families. Vartouhi became the grandmother of twelve (including a doctor) and the great-grandmother of thirty-two (and another doctor—as if to spite me!).

As for me, I endured the playful scorn of my colleagues. They said I was losing my touch. I reminded them that none of us had won the bet after all. Vartouhi made certain that she'd meet me on her own terms.

When I finally came for eighty-four-year-old Vartouhi in the hospital ward, she welcomed me like a dear friend. Esophageal cancer, of course—isn't it funny how life works?

Acknowledgments

I am deeply thankful to my MFA cohort and the faculty at the University of Michigan. This book wouldn't be possible without their editorial guidance and steadfast friendship. I am particularly grateful to my mentor, Nicholas Delbanco, and fellow writers Kristiana Kahakauwila, Andrea Lochen, and Rebecca Adams Wright, all of whom have left an indelible mark on these stories. Heartfelt thanks to Greg Schutz, Ray McDaniel, and Brad Wetherell, who were instrumental in shaping the final manuscript. Many thanks to Andrea Beauchamp and the Hopwood Program. I'm indebted to Courtland Keteyian for providing medical expertise (any mistakes are fully my own) and for sharing his great-grandmother's story. My wonderful editor, Carmen Johnson, lent her insight and editorial precision, which combined to make this book a reality.

I am also grateful for the support of Dzanc as well as the Sozopol Fiction Seminars. Also thanks to my early teachers at Iowa, especially Gallaudet Howard, for her encouragement and support. Thanks to Mustafa Samiwala and Mihos Jones, my unwavering friends.

The voracious readers of my mother's family—my grandmother Marguerite and my aunt Sandra—valued books above all else. My grandfather Lloyd called me a writer before I had the courage to do so myself. Their influence is immeasurable and I miss them dearly.

Words aren't adequate to express my gratitude to Caleb, always my first reader. And finally, to my parents—without whom, nothing.